JUSTICE LEAGUE UNLIMITED

GIRL POWER

Superman created by
Jerry Siegel and Joe Shuster.
Supergirl based on the characters
created by Jerry Siegel and Joe Shuster.
By special arrangement with the Jerry Siegel family.

KC CARLSON
RACHEL GLUCKSTERN
STEVE WACKER
MICHAEL WRIGHT
DAN RASPLER
TOM PALMER JR.
Editors - Original Series

FRANK BERRIOS
Assistant Editor - Original Series

ROBIN WILDMAN
Editor - Collected Edition

STEVE COOK
Design Director - Books

AMIE BROCKWAY-METCALF
Publication Design

CHRISTY SAWYER
Publication Production

MARIE JAVINS
Editor-in-Chief, DC Comics

DANIEL CHERRY III
Senior VP - General Manager

JIM LEE
Publisher & Chief Creative Officer

JOEN CHOE
VP - Global Brand & Creative Services

DON FALLETTI
VP - Manufacturing Operations & Workflow Management

LAWRENCE GANEM
VP - Talent Services

ALISON GILL
Senior VP - Manufacturing & Operations

NICK J. NAPOLITANO
VP - Manufacturing Administration & Design

NANCY SPEARS
VP - Revenue

JUSTICE LEAGUE UNLIMITED: GIRL POWER

DC Comics, 2900 West Alameda Ave., Burbank, CA 91505
Printed by LSC Communications, Crawfordsville, IN, USA. 5/28/21. First Printing.
ISBN: 978-1-77951-015-0

Library of Congress Cataloging-in-Publication Data is available.

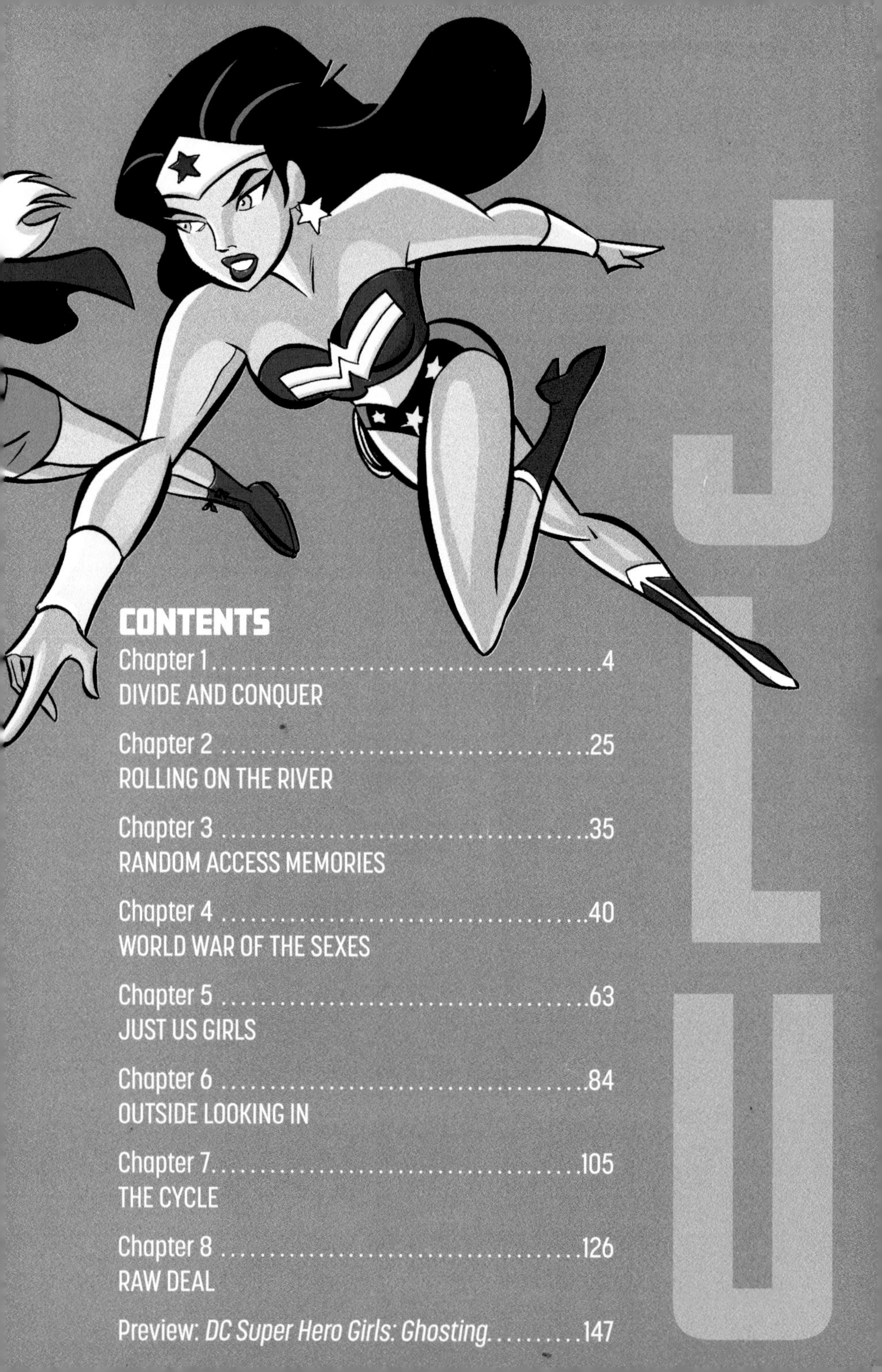

CONTENTS

JUSTICE LEAGUE UNLIMITED

DIVIDE & CONQUER
ADAM BEECHEN-WRITER • CARLO BARBERI-PENCILLER • WALDEN WONG-INKER
HEROIC AGE-COLORS • NICK J. NAPOLITANO-LETTERS • TOM PALMER JR.-EDITOR
WHAT BETTER WAY TO BEGIN THE FIRST ISSUE OF JUSTICE LEAGUE UNLIMITED--
WE HAVE NO OTHER CHOICE!
WE QUIT!
--THAN WITH THE END?
Roll Call:
Superman, Wonder Woman, Batman, Flash, Hawkgirl, Captain Atom, Zatanna

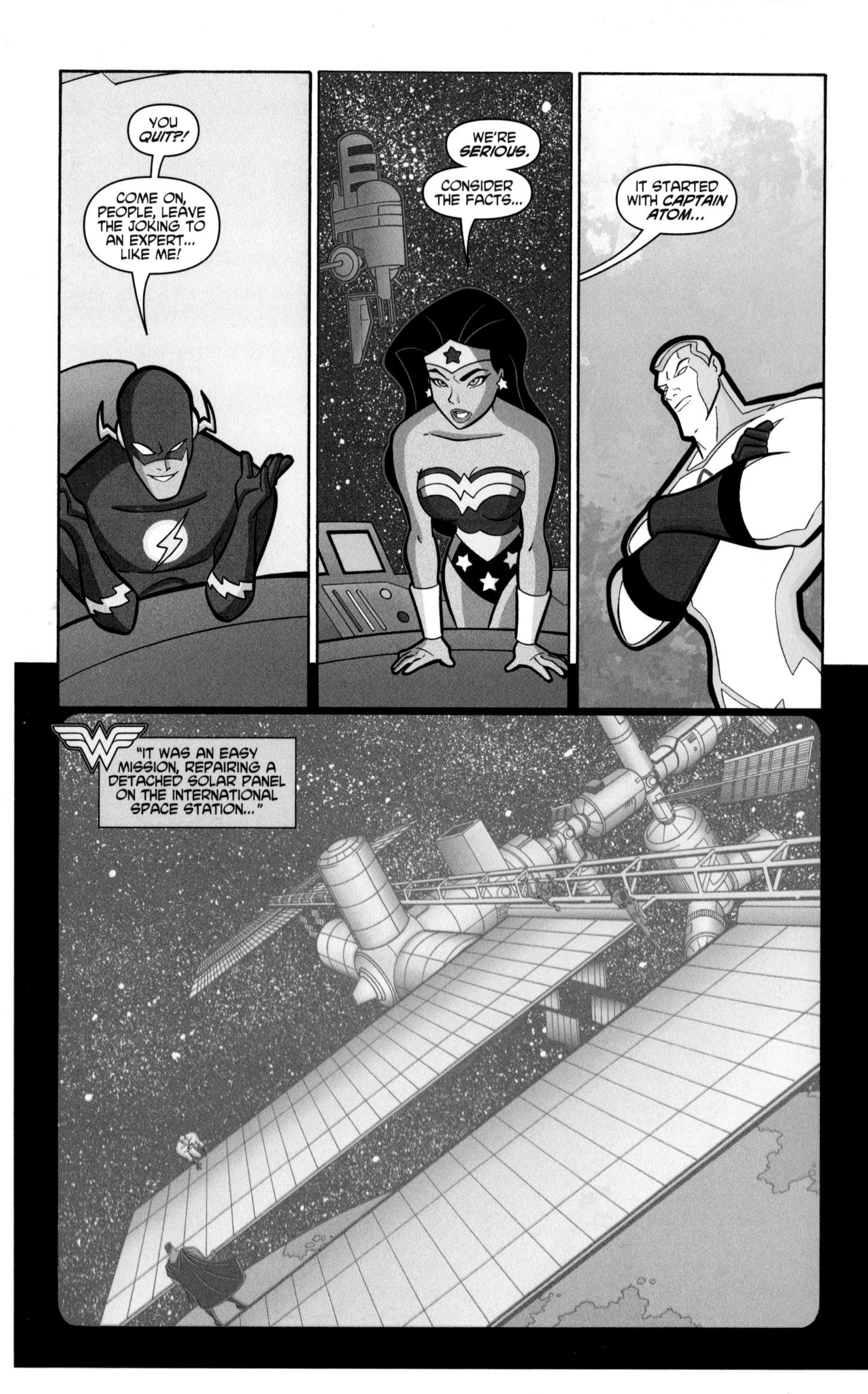
YOU QUIT?!
COME ON, PEOPLE, LEAVE THE JOKING TO AN EXPERT... LIKE ME!
WE'RE SERIOUS.
CONSIDER THE FACTS...
IT STARTED WITH CAPTAIN ATOM...
"IT WAS AN EASY MISSION, REPAIRING A DETACHED SOLAR PANEL ON THE INTERNATIONAL SPACE STATION..."

"BUT SOMETHING WENT WRONG.
"CAPTAIN ATOM TURNED AGAINST US, WITH NO WARNING, AND WITHOUT ANY REASON WE COULD SEE!
"IT TOOK ALL OF OUR STRENGTH JUST TO RESTRAIN HIM...
"AND THEN CAPTAIN ATOM WAS BACK TO NORMAL, JUST AS SUDDENLY AS HE'D GONE BERSERK.
"HE DIDN'T REMEMBER ANYTHING ABOUT HIS RAMPAGE."
WONDER WOMAN AND I BROUGHT CAPTAIN ATOM BACK HERE TO THE WATCHTOWER...

"WE DETECTED NOTHING IN OUR COMPLETE MEDICAL SCANS OF CAPTAIN ATOM...
"NO KNOWN ILLNESSES, VIRUSES OR ALIEN PRESENCES, NOTHING IMPLANTED, AND NO RECORD OF ANY THOUGHT-CONTROL TRANSMISSIONS TO HIS BRAIN ON KNOWN FREQUENCIES...
"WE WERE ABOUT TO CHALK IT UP AS AN ISOLATED FREAK INCIDENT...
"...WHEN WONDER WOMAN WENT WILD.
"I WAS NO MATCH FOR HER AMAZON MIGHT, AND CAPTAIN ATOM COULD BARELY HOLD HIS OWN..."

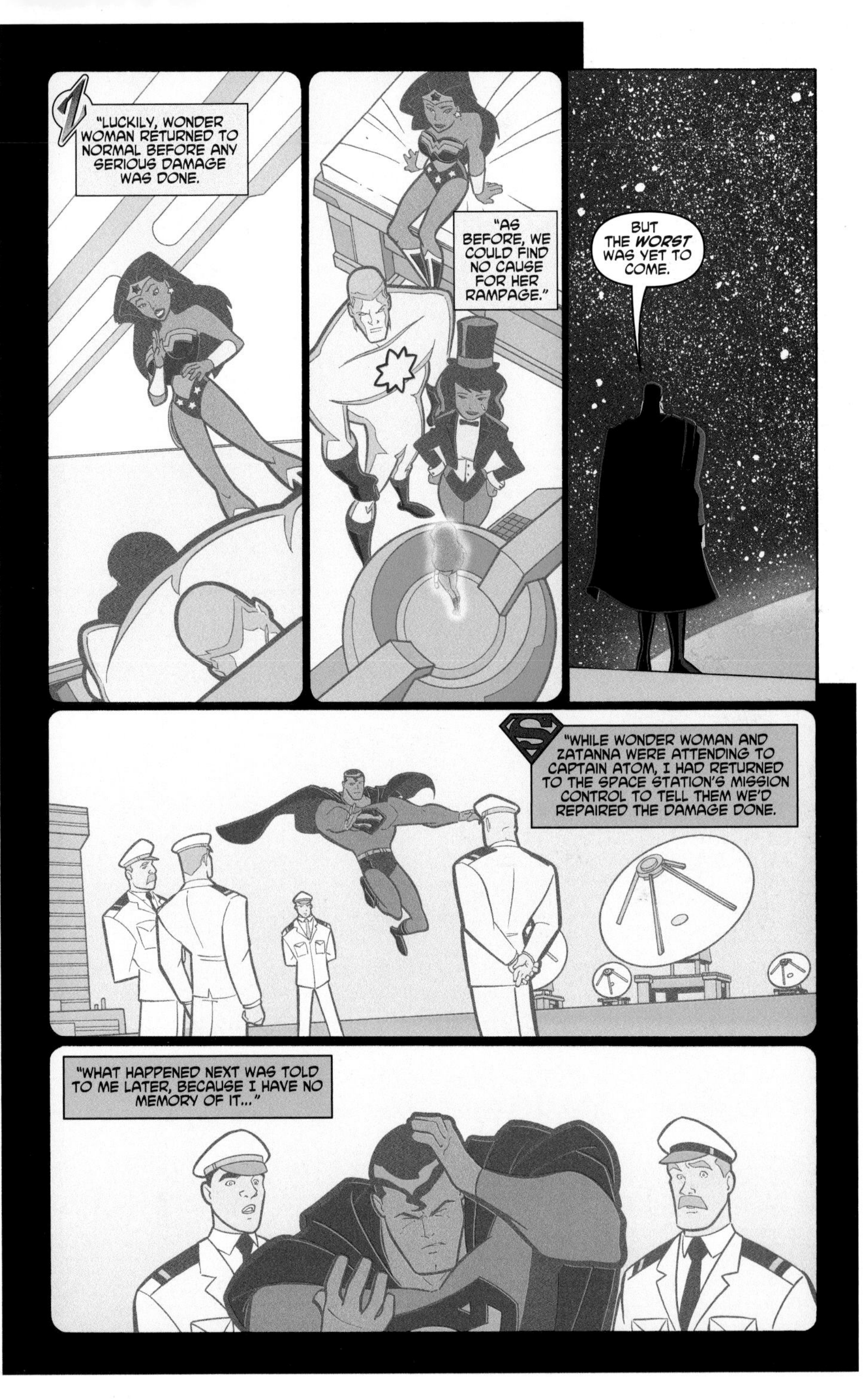
"LUCKILY, WONDER WOMAN RETURNED TO NORMAL BEFORE ANY SERIOUS DAMAGE WAS DONE.
"AS BEFORE, WE COULD FIND NO CAUSE FOR HER RAMPAGE."
BUT THE WORST WAS YET TO COME.
"WHILE WONDER WOMAN AND ZATANNA WERE ATTENDING TO CAPTAIN ATOM, I HAD RETURNED TO THE SPACE STATION'S MISSION CONTROL TO TELL THEM WE'D REPAIRED THE DAMAGE DONE.
"WHAT HAPPENED NEXT WAS TOLD TO ME LATER, BECAUSE I HAVE NO MEMORY OF IT..."

"THE PERSONNEL AT MISSION CONTROL SAID I WAS LIKE AN *ANIMAL,* FOCUSED ON NOTHING EXCEPT DESTROYING *ANYTHING* I COULD GET MY HANDS ON.
"THANK KRYPTON THAT DIDN'T INCLUDE HUMAN LIFE.
"THE SOLDIERS COULDN'T STOP ME. THEY COULDN'T EVEN TRY. USING THEIR WEAPONS AGAINST ME WOULD BE LIKE THROWING PEBBLES AT A TORNADO.
"SO THEY DID THE ONLY THING THEY COULD..."

"THEY CALLED IN THE JUSTICE LEAGUE.
"ZATANNA, WONDER WOMAN, CAPTAIN ATOM...
"THEY WERE NO MATCH FOR ME. NO ONE COULD HAVE BEEN.
"AND THEN, AS IF ONE SUPERHERO OUT OF CONTROL WASN'T ENOUGH..."

"IT LASTED FOR HALF AN HOUR. THREE OF THE MIGHTIEST BEINGS ALIVE, TURNED INTO FORCES OF DESTRUCTION."

"AND WHEN IT WAS OVER...
"...ALL WE COULD DO WAS BE GRATEFUL IT HADN'T BEEN WORSE."
WE RAN ALL THE SAME TESTS ON SUPERMAN THAT WE RAN ON WONDER WOMAN AND ME, BUT WE DIDN'T REALLY EXPECT TO FIND ANYTHING...
...AND WE DIDN'T.
THERE'S SOMETHING ABOUT THIS I DON'T GET...
WHATEVER IT WAS THAT HAPPENED ONLY AFFECTED CAPTAIN ATOM, WONDER WOMAN, AND SUPERMAN...
...BUT ZATANNA WAS THERE FOR EACH RAMPAGE, TOO!
WHY WEREN'T YOU AFFECTED, Z?
WE WONDERED THE SAME THING. WE RAN TESTS ON ME, TO SEE IF THERE WERE ANY UNUSUAL READINGS, OR IF I WAS SOMEHOW THE CAUSE OF THE OTHERS' PROBLEMS.
WE COULDN'T FIND ANYTHING.
I THINK THE REASON WHY ZATANNA WASN'T AFFECTED IS FAIRLY OBVIOUS, FLASH...

SHE'S NOT AS PHYSICALLY POWERFUL AS THE OTHERS.
NO KIDDING...

NONE OF *US* ARE. AND NONE OF US WERE TARGETED.

TARGETED? BATMAN, WHAT ARE YOU TRYING TO SAY?

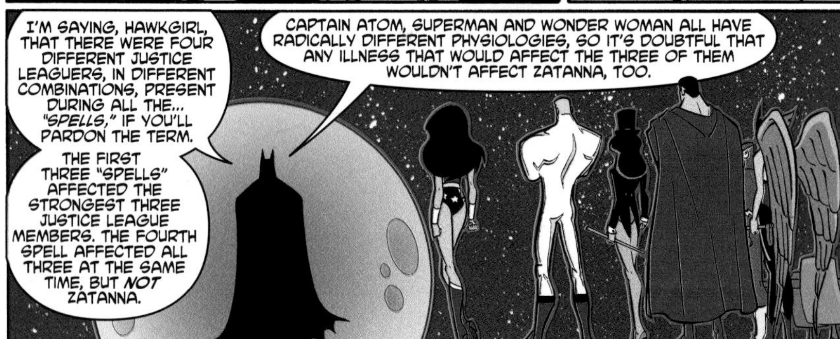
I'M SAYING, HAWKGIRL, THAT THERE WERE FOUR DIFFERENT JUSTICE LEAGUERS, IN DIFFERENT COMBINATIONS, PRESENT DURING ALL THE... *"SPELLS,"* IF YOU'LL PARDON THE TERM.
THE FIRST THREE "SPELLS" AFFECTED THE STRONGEST THREE JUSTICE LEAGUE MEMBERS. THE FOURTH SPELL AFFECTED ALL THREE AT THE SAME TIME, BUT *NOT* ZATANNA.
CAPTAIN ATOM, SUPERMAN AND WONDER WOMAN ALL HAVE RADICALLY DIFFERENT PHYSIOLOGIES, SO IT'S DOUBTFUL THAT ANY ILLNESS THAT WOULD AFFECT THE THREE OF THEM WOULDN'T AFFECT ZATANNA, TOO.

THEREFORE, WE CAN ASSUME WE'RE NOT DEALING WITH AN ILLNESS.
WE'RE UNDER ATTACK.

BUT WE DIDN'T JUST LOOK FOR ILLNESSES, REMEMBER?
WE DIDN'T FIND ANY SIGNS OF TRANSMISSIONS INTO THEIR MINDS, NO SIGNS OF POST-HYPNOTIC SUGGESTION... NOTHING!
ZATANNA EVEN SAID A FEW WORDS BACKWARDS, RAN SOME OF HER MAGIC SPELLS TO SEE IF WE WERE UNDER THE INFLUENCE OF SORCERY... NO GO.

JUST BECAUSE YOU CAN'T SEE SOMETHING...
...DOESN'T MEAN IT ISN'T THERE.

ALL OF THIS IS IRRELEVANT!
KRUNCH

YIKES!

IF THREE OF THE STRONGEST BEINGS ON EARTH CAN BE POSSESSED WITH MINDLESS, VIOLENT IMPULSES AT ANY TIME...

THEN WE'RE A DANGER TO THE ENTIRE WORLD... AND EVERYONE ON IT.

THEREFORE, WE'RE GETTING AS FAR AWAY FROM POPULATED AREAS... AND EACH OTHER... AS POSSIBLE. AT LEAST UNTIL OUR "SEIZURES" STOP HAPPENING, OR WE FIND A WAY TO *CURE* THEM.

I'VE LOCATED A DESERTED ASTEROID 4.7 LIGHT-YEARS AWAY. I'M HEADED THERE.
SUPERMAN HAS ALLOWED ME TO STAY AT HIS ARCTIC FORTRESS OF SOLITUDE.
I'M HEADED TO THE SOUTH POLE.

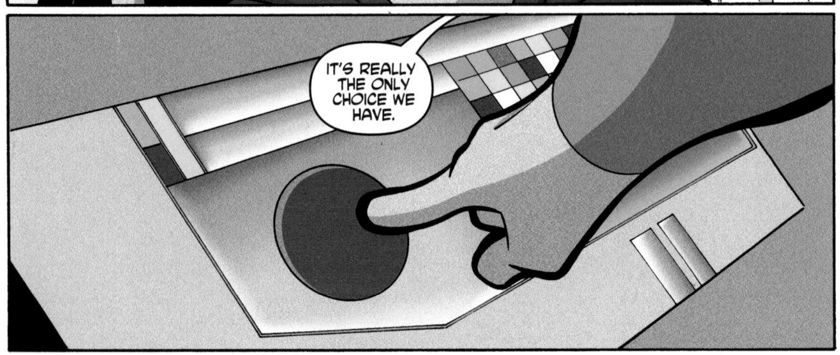
IT'S REALLY THE ONLY CHOICE WE HAVE.

NO!

WE'RE THE JUSTICE LEAGUE! WE'RE A TEAM!
WE HELP EACH OTHER, WE DON'T RUN FROM A CHALLENGE TO THE ENDS OF THE UNIVERSE!

WHAT DO YOU PROPOSE, HAWKGIRL?

I DON'T KNOW.

UNTIL WE HAVE SOME BETTER IDEAS, THIS IS THE BEST OPTION WE HAVE.
IT'S THE *ONLY* OPTION WE HAVE.

GOOD LUCK.

WELL...

I GUESS WE SHOULD PLACE A *"HELP WANTED"* AD...

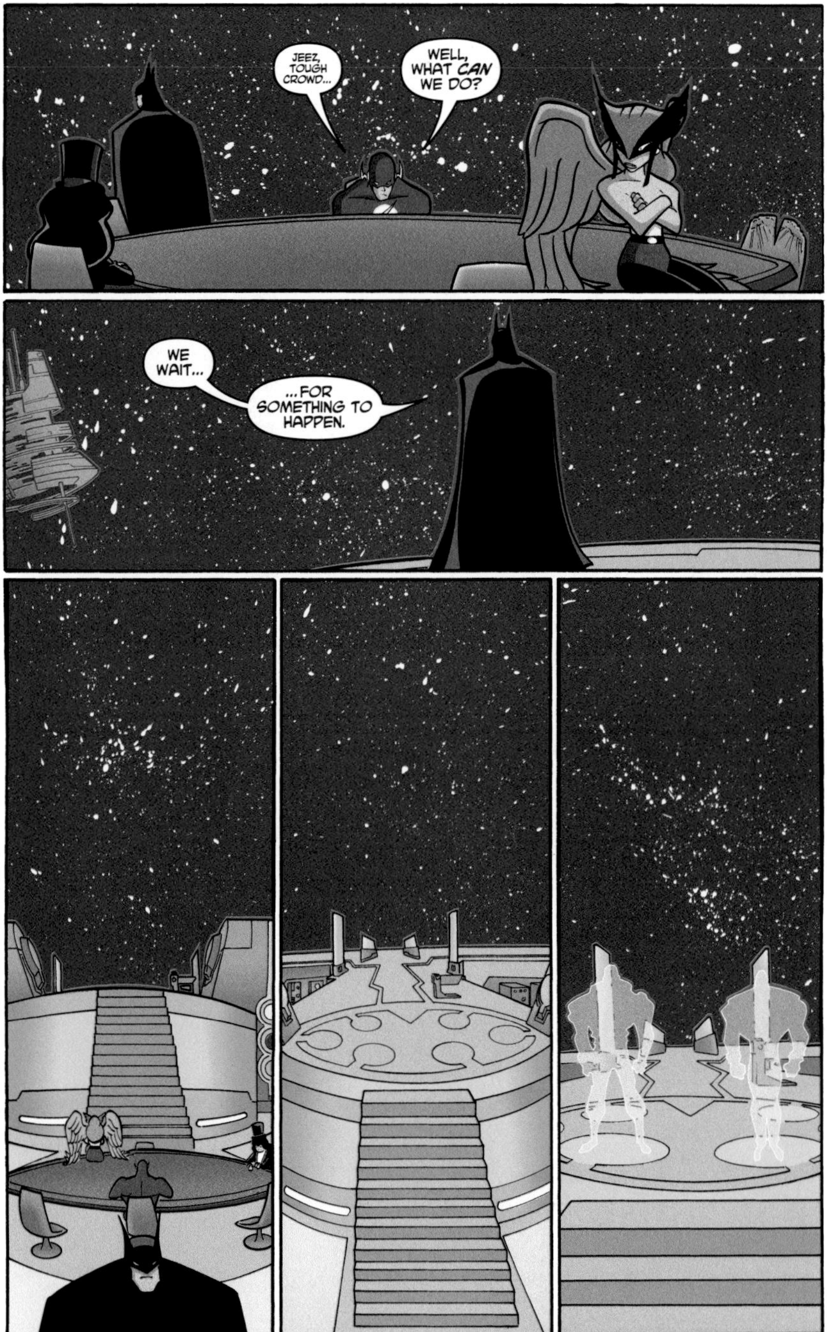

JEEZ, TOUGH CROWD...
WELL, WHAT *CAN* WE DO?
WE WAIT...
...FOR SOMETHING TO HAPPEN.

HELLO.
WE'RE THE NEW LAND-LORDS.

DESPERO! BRAINIAC!
GET THEM!

MAMMALS, BE STILL.
WE ARE AS THE WOMAN NAMED US. AND WE ARE YOUR BETTERS.

OUR NAMES SOUND GOOD TOGETHER, DON'T THEY? I DON'T KNOW WHY WE DIDN'T JOIN TOGETHER SOONER...
BRAINIAC, A SUPER-COMPUTER WITH COMPLETE KNOWLEDGE OF EVERYTHING IN *YOUR* GALAXY...
AND ME, WITH KNOWLEDGE OF EVERYTHING FROM THE GALAXY OF *MY* PLANET, KALANOR...

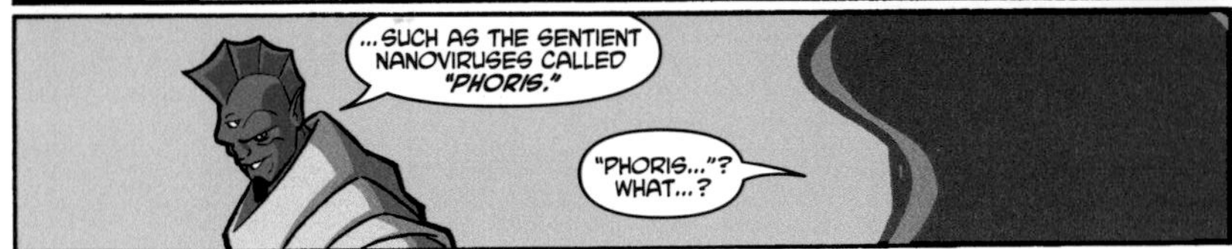
...SUCH AS THE SENTIENT NANOVIRUSES CALLED *"PHORIS."*
"PHORIS..."? WHAT...?

YOU'VE NEVER ENCOUNTERED THE PHORIS BEFORE, SO YOU WOULDN'T EVEN KNOW HOW TO LOOK FOR THEM.
LOVELY CREATURES. THEY CAN BE TAUGHT TO ADAPT TO UNIQUE PHYSIOLOGIES, AND ONCE INSIDE A HOST, THE PHORIS RENDER THEM VERY... AGREEABLE.
BRAINIAC AND I HAVE BEEN HIDING IN MY SHIP, CLOAKED, IN YOUR ORBIT FOR DAYS, PUMPING THE PHORIS INTO YOUR VENTILATION SYTEM.
THEY'LL ONLY STAY IN YOUR BODIES A FEW DAYS MORE, AND THEY'RE HARMLESS IF THEY'RE NOT CONTROLLED...
BUT WITH ONE CLICK OF THIS, WE CAN MAKE YOUR DEPARTED FRIENDS... OR YOU... DO ANYTHING WE WANT.
IN FACT, IN A MOMENT, WE'RE GOING TO MAKE THEM DESTROY YOUR PLANET WHILE BRAINIAC ABSORBS EVERY OUNCE OF DATA IN YOUR COMPUTERS.
AND... AND US?
OH, NONE OF YOU ARE POWERFUL ENOUGH TO BE OF ANY USE TO US. WE'RE GOING TO DESTROY YOU OURSELVES.
WHAT DO YOU SAY TO THAT?

NOISULLI EDAF.

THAT'S WHAT I HAVE TO SAY.

BRAINIAC, DESPERO...
ENOUGH IS ENOUGH!

NO! NO! BRAINIAC, IT WAS ALL AN ILLUSION!
THEY KNEW WE'D BE MONITORING THEM, WAITING FOR THEIR MOST MIGHTY TO LEAVE! IT WAS A TRICK TO GET US TO REVEAL OURSELVES!
BUT WE ARE NOT DEFEATED! NOT WHILE WE STILL HAVE THE PHORIS!
RELLORTNOC OTNI SREWOLF

JUSTICE LEAGUE...TAKE THEM DOWN!
FOOL OF A HUMAN. I HAVE ALL THE KNOWLEDGE IN YOUR COMPUTERS...
MORE THAN ENOUGH TO DESTROY YOU!
IS THAT SO? THEN YOUR CIRCUITS MUST BE PRETTY FULL, BRAINIAC!
I WONDER WHAT'LL HAPPEN IF I OVERLOAD YOU WITH ATOMIC ENERGY?
EEEEEEEEEEE
TOO BAD FOR YOUR SCHEME, DESPERO...
...LOOKS LIKE THE "PHORIS" IS NO LONGER WITH YOU!

BATMAN, YOUR PLAN... IT WORKED *PERFECTLY!*
ACTUALLY, ZATANNA, AFTER DESPERO AND BRAINIAC MADE THEIR FATAL MISTAKE, CONCEIVING THE PLAN WAS RELATIVELY SIMPLE...

I KNOW I'M GONNA FEEL STUPID FOR ASKING THIS...
...BUT WHAT WAS THEIR FATAL MISTAKE?

IT WAS THEIR BELIEF THAT, BY ELIMINATING THE LEAGUE'S "STRONGEST MEMBERS," THEY HAD WON.
THEY'D FORGOTTEN SOMETHING WE'VE KNOWN ALL ALONG...

IN THE JUSTICE LEAGUE, THERE *ARE* NO WEAK LINKS.
END

...EXPERIMENTAL WEAPONS STOLEN FROM A RUSSIAN LAB. WE GOT A TIP THAT THE GANG WHO HIJACKED THE SHIPMENT FROM MR. D'S MOB IS BRINGING THEM IN ON THAT FREIGHTER.
THEY PLAN TO USE ALL THAT FIREPOWER TO BUST SOME SUPERVILLAINS OUT OF BELLE REVE PRISON!
WE'LL TRY TO NAIL 'EM AS SOON AS THEY DOCK-- NOT GIVE 'EM A CHANCE TO BRING THOSE BIG GUNS INTO PLAY! BUT JUST IN CASE ANYTHING GOES WRONG...
...THAT'S WHY YOU ASKED ME TO THIS PARTY.
CAPTAIN! OUT ON THE RIVER-- LOOK!
PORT OF NE

"WHAT'S THAT FOOL DOING? HE'LL RUIN EVERYTHING! DIDN'T SOMEONE TELL THE RIVER PATROL ABOUT THIS OPERATION?!"
ahoy! DIDN'T YOU SEE THAT MARKER BUOY BACK THERE? YOU PASSED ON THE WRONG SIDE!
NEW ORLEANS RIVER PATROL
RP

THAT'S A VIOLATION OF ORDINANCE 38.4, SECTION B!
I'M GOING TO HAVE TO COME ABOARD AND INSPECT YOUR CARGO!
"THIS CAN'T BE HAPPENING!"

HEAR THAT? THE MAN WANTS T'SEE OUR CARGO!
NO PROBLEMO-- I'LL GIVE HIM A REAL CLOSE LOOK!
H-HOLD IT RIGHT THERE...

"uh-oh!--
"--THIS LOOKS LIKE A JOB FOR--
KRA-KOW!

POWER GIRL
ROLLING on the RIVER
I'M ON IT, CAPTAIN! SEE IF YOU CAN DRAW THE ATTENTION OF THOSE TRIGGER-HAPPY THUGS -- THAT PATROLMAN IN THE WATER IS A SITTING DUCK!
YOU HEARD THE LADY! LET'S GIVE SOME COVERING FIRE!
BLAM!
BLAM!
KA-POW!
BAM!
BAM!
STEVE VANCE · JOHN DELANEY · RON BOYD
SCRIPT PENCILS INKS
TIM HARKINS · BOB LE ROSE · FRANK BERRIOS
LETTERS COLORS ASS'T EDITS
KC CARLSON - MISSION CONTROL
2

SO THE COPS ARE THROWING A SUPERHERO AT US, huh? WELL, THAT JUST MEANS WE GET T' BREAK OUT THE REAL FIREWORKS A LITTLE SOONER THAN I PLANNED!
GET BUSY ON THOSE CRATES --!
VOOM!
VOOM!
--WE'LL SHOW POWER BABE WHAT POWER REALLY MEANS!
HANG ON, PAL!
POWER G--
VOOM! KA-POW!
VOOM! BRATTATATTAT!
--UURRK!
YOU MAY BE RESPONSIBLE FOR THIS MESS...
...BUT THAT DOESN'T MEAN I'M GOING TO LET THEM BLAST YOU TO BITS!
NOW SEE IF YOU CAN AVOID CAUSING ANY MORE TROUBLE FOR AWHILE!
I WAS JUST TRYING TO-TO...
...DO MY JOB...
3

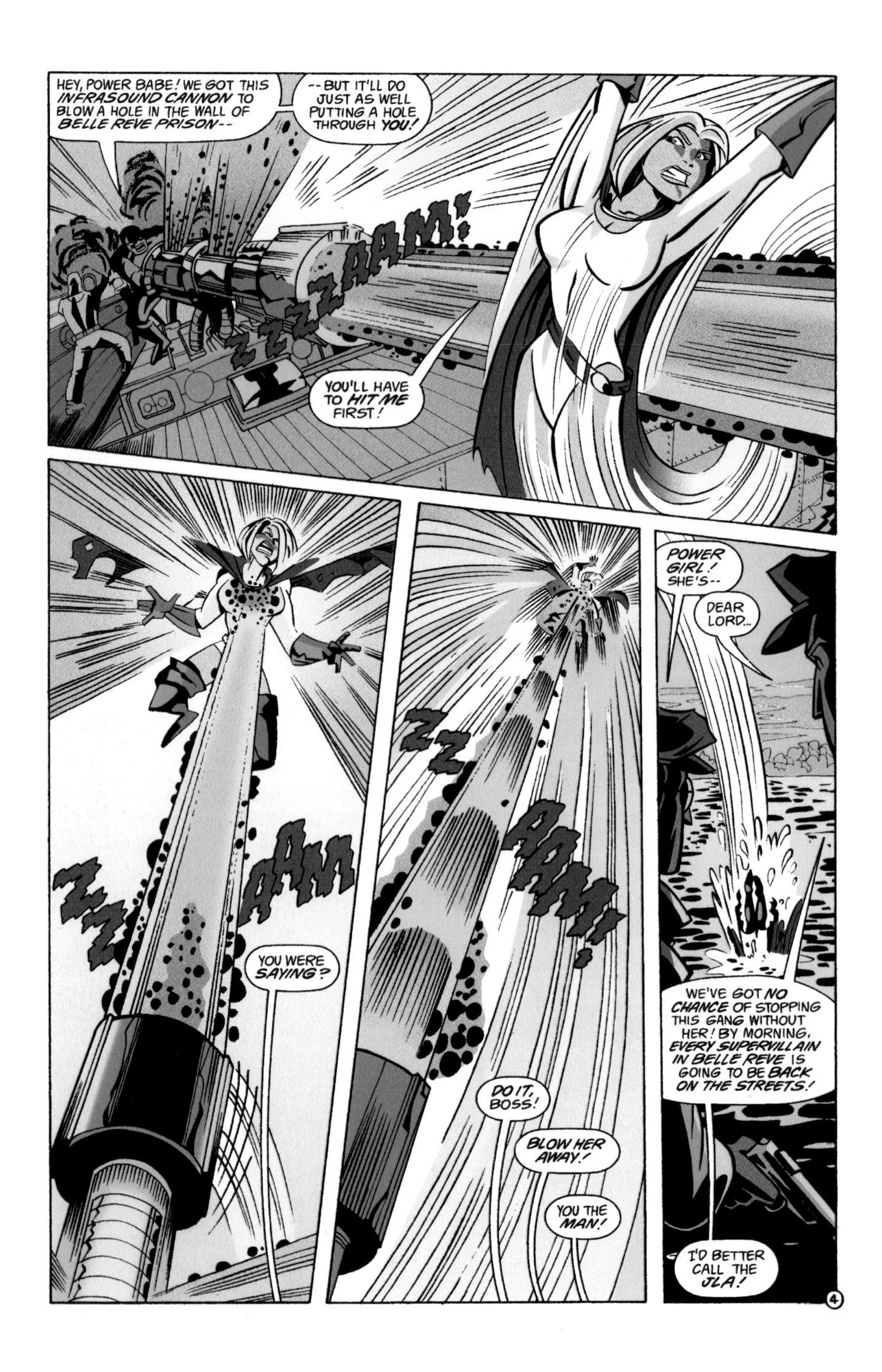
HEY, POWER BABE! WE GOT THIS INFRASOUND CANNON TO BLOW A HOLE IN THE WALL OF BELLE REVE PRISON--
--BUT IT'LL DO JUST AS WELL PUTTING A HOLE THROUGH YOU!
ZZZZZAAAM!
YOU'LL HAVE TO HIT ME FIRST!
ZZZAAAM!
YOU WERE SAYING?
ZZAAM!
DO IT, BOSS!
BLOW HER AWAY!
YOU THE MAN!
POWER GIRL! SHE'S--
DEAR LORD...
WE'VE GOT NO CHANCE OF STOPPING THIS GANG WITHOUT HER! BY MORNING, EVERY SUPERVILLAIN IN BELLE REVE IS GOING TO BE BACK ON THE STREETS!
I'D BETTER CALL THE JLA!
4

"CAPTAIN--LOOK! IT'S--"

KA-POW! POW!
POWER GIRL!
SHE AIN'T DEAD!
ZZING!

SHE WILL BE--
VOOM!
KA-VOOM!

CHOOM!
--AS SOON AS I GET THIS CANNON INTO POSITION!

BLAM! KA-BLAM! POW! POW! KA-POW!
KEEP FIRING! WE'VE GOT TO PUT THAT CANNON OUT OF ACTION BEFORE IT BLASTS POWER GIRL AGAIN!

ving!
Ka-ping!
YOU'RE WASTING YOUR BULLETS, CHUMPS! THOSE POPGUNS CAN'T PENETRATE THIS SHIELD!

BUT I CAN, CREEP!
5

WOO! YOU'RE CUTE WHEN YOU'RE MAD!
ZZZZZAMM!
ZZ ZAAAAM!
DON'T GIVE UP! THIS THING'S GONNA RUN OUT OF POWER--
--IN ABOUT TWO HOURS! THINK YOU CAN LAST THAT LONG?
DON'T KNOW--IF I CAN LAST --TWO MORE MINUTES!
MAYBE I CAN PUNCH MY WAY INTO THE SHIP-- GET OUT OF THE LINE OF FIRE! GOT TO TRY--!
BANG! BANG!
GIVE IT UP, GIRL! YOU'RE JUST--
--WHA?!
BANG!
AAAHH! I'M HIT! THAT LITTLE CREEP SHOT ME!
STOP WHINING--
6

--OR I'LL DO THIS TO YOU, NOT JUST TO YOUR TOY!
KRUNCH!
URK!
SORRY I WAS A LITTLE ROUGH WITH YOU EARLIER-- I WAS LUCKY YOU WERE THERE, AS IT TURNED OUT. YOU'RE QUITE A MARKSMAN.
ACTUALLY, I'M THE LUCKY ONE! I WAS JUST TRYING TO DISTRACT THAT GUY-- I NEVER THOUGHT I'D HIT HIM!
I'VE FLUNKED THE N.O.P.D.'S PISTOL TEST THREE TIMES-- THAT'S WHY I'M A RIVER COP!
SON, I'M GOING TO GET YOU A TUTOR-- WE'LL MAKE SURE YOU PASS NEXT TIME!
I'VE BROUGHT IN OUR INFORMANT-- I'M HOPING HE CAN HELP US IDENTIFY SOME OF THESE THUGS.
BEFORE HE MADE A DEAL WITH THE FEDS TODAY, FRED HERE WAS CHIEF ACCOUNTANT FOR MR. D'S MOB.
WHOEVER STOLE THESE WEAPONS FROM MR. D HAD TO HAVE AN INSIDE MAN. MR. D. THOUGHT IT WAS ME-- BUT I WAS SET UP!
HE DIDN'T BELIEVE ME! 13 YEARS I'VE WORKED FOR HIM! HE TRIED TO--
-- WELL, LET'S JUST SAY THAT HIS HANDLING OF THE MATTER LEFT ME WITH NO FURTHER FEELING OF LOYALTY TO HIM.
NOW LET'S SEE WHO...
BASIL!
ULP! FRED!
HAHAHAHAHA! I CAN'T TELL YOU HOW HAPPY I AM TO SEE YOU!
WHAT'S SO FUNNY?
THE FBI CAUGHT MR. D AND HIS #1 BOY OMAR TRYING TO SNEAK INTO THE COUNTRY A FEW HOURS AGO. NOW THEY'LL ALL BE DOING TIME TOGETHER--
--SO MR. D CAN PERSONALLY "THANK" BASIL FOR DOUBLE-CROSSING HIM!
I'D AVOID WET CEMENT IF I WERE YOU, BASIL-- AND STAY OUT OF THE PRISON SWIMMING POOL!
THE END

JLU

UGGH! ANOTHER BEAUTIFUL NIGHT IN GOTHAM! PERFECT WEATHER --TO BE SOMEWHERE ELSE!
IF THAT TIP ABOUT A MICROCHIP HEIST TURNS OUT TO BE A FALSE ALARM, MY INFORMANT WILL BE SORRY!
CAN'T SEE A THING IN THIS RAIN. I'D BETTER CHECK IT OUT--

--FROM THE INSIDE.
YOU'RE TOO LATE, BLACK CANARY
RANDOM ACCESS MEMORIES!
PROGRAMMING BY:
STEVE VANCE-SCRIPT JOHN DELANEY-PENCILS
RON BOYD-INKS TIM HARKINS-LETTERING
BOB LE ROSE-COLORS FRANK BERRIOS-ASS'T. EDITS
KC CARLSON - MR. MAINFRAME

WHO--?
GASP
I'M PORTER CULLIS. THIS IS MY COMPANY-- OR AT LEAST IT WAS.

I'D BETTER GET YOU TO A DOCTOR!
NO TIME. "THE HAMMER" LEFT ME FOR DEAD--AND HE WASN'T FAR WRONG.

ED "THE HAMMER" HAMILTON--THE UNDERWORLD MUSCLE-MAN? HOW DID YOU GET MIXED UP WITH HIM?
I-I BORROWED MONEY--FROM THE WRONG PEOPLE.
WE'VE DESIGNED A NEW MICROCHIP. IT'S AWESOME--ANYBODY WHO SEES IT, IT'LL KNOCK THEIR SOCKS OFF. IT'S WORTH MILLIONS.

--IF WE CAN FINISH THE PROTOTYPE. I WAS DESPERATE--TRYING TO KEEP MY BUSINESS GOING UNTIL IT PAID OFF.
I HOOKED UP WITH A FIXER NAMED MO MENDEL. THEY CALL HIM --
--"MENTAL MORRIE"! AND WHEN YOU COULDN'T PAY, HE SENT IN THE HAMMER!

IT'S WORSE THAN THAT! MENTAL MORRIE STOLE THE CHIP DESIGN!
YOU'VE GOT TO STOP HIM! YOU CAN'T LET HIM GET THE CREDIT FOR IT! IT'S ALL I'VE GOT--
--IT'S WHAT I'LL BE REMEMBERED FOR...

HOW IS MORRIE TRANSPORTING THE CHIP SPECS--CD? DAT TAPE?
Nah. HE JUST READ 'EM--THE WHOLE 130 PAGES. HE'S GOT A PHOTOGRAPHIC MEMORY.

-KOFF- IT'S ALL IN HIS HEAD NOW! NO WAY TO RETRIEVE IT!
HE DRIVES A BLACK BMW--JERSEY PLATES--PROBABLY HEADING FOR THE AIRPORT!

"PROMISE ME YOU'LL GET 'EM, WILL Y--"
"-KOFF KOFF-
"CULLIS? PORTER?!"
@#%*!! DEAD AS A DOORNAIL!
"I PROMISE, PORTER."
2

NEXT TIME I STEAL A CAR, I'M CHECKIN' THE MAINTENANCE RECORDS FIRST!
WE'LL NEVER GET A TAXI IN THIS WEATHER! COME ON--
GOTHAM TRANSIT
SUBWAY
SUBWAY
--WE'LL HAVE TO RESORT TO PUBLIC TRANS-PORTATION.
WHAT NOW, MORRIE?
137
THE NEXT "D" TRAIN IS DUE IN SIX MINUTES. IT SHOULD GET US TO GOTHAM CENTRAL STATION AT 2:04.
FROM THERE, WE CAN GET A TAXI TO THE AIRPORT AND CATCH THE 3:40 FLIGHT TO TOKYO!
I DUNNO HOW YOU REMEMBER ALL THOSE SCHEDULES!
I CAN'T HELP BUT REMEMBER.
FORGETTING IS THE HARD PART.
HUH?
NEVER MIND...
HEY, MENTAL--
3

--YOU LEFT YOUR CAR IN A RED ZONE!
DON'T BE ABSURD-- PARKING IS LEGAL THERE FROM 7 P.M. TO 6 A.M.--
--EXCEPT TUESDA--
YOU'RE KIDDING, RIGHT?
HE DON'T JOKE, LADY!
MOM
THAT FIGURES.
WHONK!
DON'T BOTHER GETTIN' UP, CANARY--
--'CAUSE IT'S HAMMER TIME!
Oh, PUH-LEASE! DON'T TELL ME WE'RE REVIVING THAT ONE ALREADY.
NEXT YOU'LL BE SAYING "WHOOMP, THERE IT IS!"
4

SMEK!
YOU KILLED A MAN TONIGHT, HAMMER. A NICE GUY. SMART-- TALENTED--
WOOF!
THUNK!
SO?
SO--
KLANG!

--THIS!
SPAK!
I PROMISED HIM I'D GET YOU--
HURRFEF!
--AND I KEEP MY PROMISES!
KLUNK!
5

GOING SOMEWHERE, MORRIE?
THOOOOOOMP!
HEEELP!
STAY BACK, CANARY--I'M WARNING YOU!
AND I'M WARNING YOU, MORRIE --IF YOU HURT HER--
HERE COMES THE TRAIN! I'M GETTING ON IT, AND TAKING THE PLANS WITH ME--LOCKED UP SAFELY IN MY HEAD!
ARE YOU SURE YOU REMEMBER IT, MORRIE?
6

I REMEMBER...
...ALL OF IT...
...I CAN'T FORGET...
...ANYTHING...
WHA--?
LIKE PORTER SAID--"ANYBODY WHO SEES IT, IT'LL KNOCK THEIR SOCKS OFF."
CLOSE ENOUGH.
END

JUSTICE LEAGUE UNLIMITED

SUPERMAN. WONDER WOMAN. BATMAN. GREEN LANTERN. FLASH. HAWKGIRL. THE MARTIAN MANHUNTER. WHEN THE WORLD IS IN DEADLY DANGER AND A SINGLE HERO IS NOT ENOUGH, THEY WILL RISE TO VICTORY, LEAVING JUSTICE IN THEIR WAKE.
The JUSTICE LEAGUE in
World War of the SEXES
WELL STRUCK, SISTER!
BY HERA, WHAT A BLOW!
YOU MUST BE PROUD, YOUR MAJESTY!
YOUR DAUGHTER TRULY IS A WONDER WOMAN...
writer: Dan Slott pencils: Min S. Ku inks: Rob Leigh color: John Kalisz letters: Hathaway seps: Heroic Age ass't ed: Steve Wacker editor: Dan Raspler

...AND AN INSPIRATION TO US ALL!
AYE, SHE IS. IN MORE WAYS THAN I HAD BARGAINED.

"HERE ON THEMYSCIRA, WE AMAZONS HAVE LONG AVERTED OUR GAZE FROM 'MAN'S WORLD.'
"BUT NOW, FOLLOWING PRINCESS DIANA'S ADVENTURES...
"...WE HAVE SEEN TEASING GLIMPSES OF WHAT LIES BEYOND OUR ISLAND PARADISE."

FARAWAY LANDS! NEW CHALLENGES! HOW EXCITING IT ALL MUST BE!
WHO KNOWS, MAYBE SOME-DAY WE COULD--
AMAZONS, ATTEND ME!

DO NOT BE SWAYED BY THE OUTER GLAMOUR OF 'MAN'S WORLD!'
IF YOU WOULD JUDGE IT, LOOK DEEPER...

...AND SEE HOW IT TREATS YOUR MORTAL SISTERS!
HOW IT SUBJUGATES, DEGRADES, AND DOMINATES THEM!

LOOK YOU NOW UPON 'MAN'S WORLD!'
QUEEN HIPPOLYTA! WE HAD NO IDEA--
WHAT CAN WE DO?

WE CAN PRAY, SISTERS.
PRAY TO ATHENA, GODDESS OF WISDOM AND TRUTH.
PRAY FOR UNDERSTANDING.

KA-THOOM
ARISE, QUEEN OF THE AMAZONS! ARISE AND FIND THE ENLIGHTENMENT YOU SEEK!
ATHENA! BLESSED GODDESS! YOU ARE HERE!

AYE, HERE TO CHARGE YOU WITH A HEROIC TASK--

--TO FORCE PEACE UPON THE WORLD OF MAN!

THE WATCHTOWER:
ORBITAL HEADQUARTERS TO THE WORLD'S GREATEST SUPER HEROES, THE JUSTICE LEAGUE!
BY MY CALCULATIONS, IN THIRTY DAYS WE'LL BE FACING CIVIL WAR.
A WHOLE MONTH? NO SWEAT, BATS.
IN THAT TIME, I COULD CHANGE EVERY LIGHT BULB ON EARTH. TWICE!
THAT'S FACTORING IN OUR INTERVENTION, FLASH.
WE'RE TALKING ABOUT AN ARMY OF AMAZONS. EACH AS POWERFUL AS WONDER WOMAN.
THEY'VE ALREADY CONQUERED THE MEDITERRANEAN...
...AND CONVERTED EVERY LOCAL FEMALE TO THEIR CAUSE.
HOW IS THIS POSSIBLE, DIANA?
IT'S A FORM OF "SISTERHOOD MAGIC," BATMAN.

WE AMAZONS ADAPTED IT FROM ONE OF MAN'S WARTIME RITUALS.
LONG AGO IT WAS A CUSTOM...

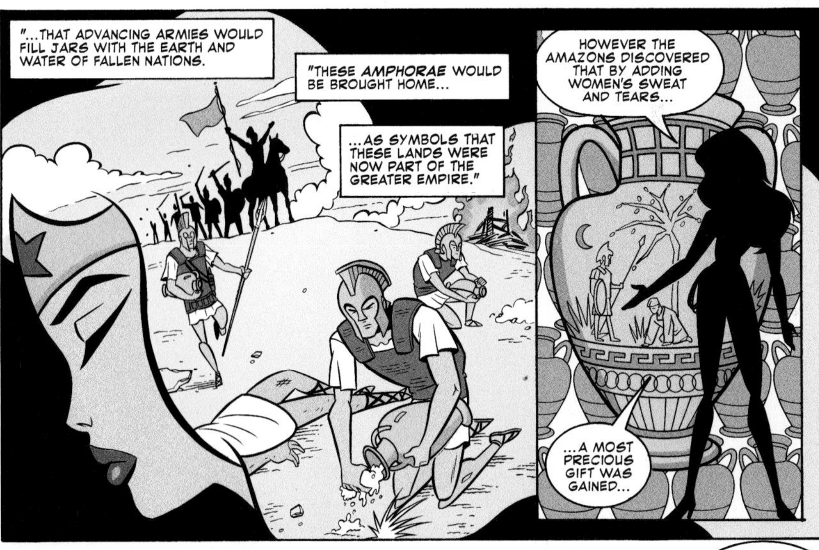
"...THAT ADVANCING ARMIES WOULD FILL JARS WITH THE EARTH AND WATER OF FALLEN NATIONS.
"THESE AMPHORAE WOULD BE BROUGHT HOME...
...AS SYMBOLS THAT THESE LANDS WERE NOW PART OF THE GREATER EMPIRE."
HOWEVER THE AMAZONS DISCOVERED THAT BY ADDING WOMEN'S SWEAT AND TEARS...
...A MOST PRECIOUS GIFT WAS GAINED...

...THE UNWAVERING LOYALTY OF EVERY WOMAN BORN TO THAT SOIL!
THANKS, WONDER WOMAN. GOOD TO KNOW. SO YOU AND HAWKGIRL WILL STAY PUT...
...WHILE THE REST OF US GO AFTER THESE JARS.

WHAT?!
YOU CAN'T BE SERIOUS, GREEN LANTERN!
THEY'RE CONTROLLING WOMEN'S MINDS, DIANA. THAT MAKES FEMALE MEMBERS A LIABILITY.
SEE? THIS IS WHY NO ONE WANTS CHICKS IN THE MILITARY.

WHY, YOU LITTLE--
MY MARTIAN SENSES VOUCH FOR HAWKGIRL!
NO OUTSIDE FORCES ARE AFFECTING HER MIND... EXCEPT FOR FLASH'S ATTEMPTS AT HUMOR.

WE'RE WASTING VALUABLE TIME.
AGREED. DIANA, TAKE J'ONN AND HAWKGIRL AND HEAD TO THEMYSCIRA.
TRY TO TALK TO YOUR MOTHER.

THE REST OF US WILL HOLD OFF THE AMAZON ARMY.
IS THAT WISE, SUPERMAN? EVEN THOUGH J'ONN IS A MARTIAN...
...HE IS STILL A MAN. HIS PRESENCE WILL NOT BE TOLERATED.

NOT UNLESS HE'S PROPERLY DRESSED FOR THE OCCASION.

AS AN ALIEN I'VE ALWAYS FELT A SORT OF KINSHIP TO SUPERMAN...
...BUT USING MY MARTIAN POWERS TO TAKE THE FORM OF HIS COUSIN IS QUITE AN ODD SENSA--
QUIET, "SUPERGIRL"! AMAZONS POSSESS A KEEN SENSE OF HEARING.
ON YOUR GUARD! ALREADY A GATHERING AWAITS OUR ARRIVAL!

HAIL MOTHER!
I TRUST I AM WELCOME?
NO, DAUGHTER, YOU MOST CERTAINLY ARE NOT!

YOU SIDE WITH THE CHAMPIONS OF MAN.
YOU'VE CHOSEN YOUR PATH. AND NOW THERE SHALL COME A RECKONING.

A DIVINE RECKONING!
KATHOOM
ATHENA!

HEAR ME, CHILD!
I OFFER YOU THIS ONE CHANCE! JOIN YOUR SISTERS AT MY SIDE!
HELP THEM OVERTHROW THE OPPRESSIVE RULE OF MAN, AND YOU SHALL BE SAVED!
MY GODDESS, I...
NO! THIS IS WRONG!
THE ATHENA I KNOW...
THE ATHENA I HOLD IN MY HEART, SHE WOULD NEVER--
BLASPHEMY! HOW DARE YOU SPEAK IN MY NAME!
BE STILL!
J'ONN, HELP! I CAN'T BREAK HER FREE!
DIANA!
GNN! IT'S NO USE!
EVEN MY INTANGIBLE FORM CANNOT PASS THROUGH THIS!
A MAN! WHAT TREACHERY IS THIS?!
SISTERS, READY YOURSELVES! THE MOMENT WE HAVE PREPARED FOR...

BEHOLD! THE BOW OF ARTEMIS, GODDESS OF THE HUNT!

SHIELD OF APOLLO, GOD OF THE SUN!

THE QURACI DESERT, HUNDREDS OF MILES TO THE EAST...
HEADS UP! ANOTHER WAVE'S COMING OVER THAT RIDGE!
IT'S WORSE THAN YOU THINK, GREEN LANTERN.
MY ENHANCED SENSES DETECT TWO MORE FLANKS BEHIND THEM!
SO? BRING IT ON! THERE'S PLENTY OF ROOM LEFT ON MY DANCE CARD!
FLASH! DON'T MAKE ME SAY IT AGAIN! THIS ISN'T A GAME!
THIS IS *WAR*!
HA! ON THEMYSCIRA OUR GAMES ARE *FAR* HARDER!
NEXT TO A ROUND OF "BULLETS AND BRACELETS," THIS *PALES* IN COMPARISON!
PANG
PANG
PANG
I'VE ALWAYS PREFERRED BRAINS OVER BULLETS, MYSELF.

MY BRACELETS! THEY'RE FUSED TOGETHER!
WHICH, AS LEGENDS GO, ROBS AN AMAZON OF HER POWERS.
IN THIS CASE, THANKS TO CHEMICALLY TREATED BATARANGS.

I WONDER IF GREEN ENERGY PLASMA CAN GET THE JOB DONE TOO?
NOT BAD!
GOOD WORK, STEWART! KEEP IT U-U-U-

AARRHH!

SUPERMAN?!
IT WAS SOME KIND OF PSYCHIC FLASH FROM J'ONN! THE OTHERS ARE IN DANGER!
NO SWEAT! I'M ON IT!

FLASH! WAIT!
IT'S NO USE. HE'S HALFWAY THERE BY NOW!

NEXT STOP, PARADISE ISLAND...
...EVERYBODY OFF.
WHOA! THAT DON'T LOOK GOOD! DON'T WORRY, KIDS.
UNCLE FLASH WILL HAVE YOU OUT OF THERE IN A JIFFY!

NOT SO FAST, LITTLE MAN!
LADY, "FAST" IS MY MIDDLE NAME.
AS IN "FLASH, THE FASTEST MAN ALIVE!"
TRUE. BUT NEXT TO A WOMAN WEARING THE SANDALS OF HERMES...
...YOU ARE HARDLY THE "FASTEST" ANYTHING!
WHAT THE--?!
WHAK WHAK WHAK
AND SOON, I DOUBT YOU'LL EVEN BE "ALIVE!"
MORE OF THEM! BUT IT DOESN'T MATTER.
THE ONLY MAN TO EVER DEFEAT ME...

...DID SO THROUGH TREACHERY!
ZZAP!
BUT NOW, ARMED WITH THE WINGS OF NIKE, GODDESS OF VICTORY..
...I AM UNBEATABLE!
AND EVEN THIS MODERN-DAY HERAKLES, THIS "SUPERMAN," WILL FALL BEFORE ME!
THWOOM
UNH!
BOY, DO I HATE MAGIC.
THE ONE CALLED GREEN LANTERN. I'VE BEEN AWAITING YOU.
IS THAT SO?
DON'T ENGAGE HER, STEWART! PICK ANOTHER--

ZZAKK
STEWART!
SPASH!

INCREDIBLE! ACCORDING TO MY RING, THIS STUFF IS PURE SOLAR ENERGY...
...WITH THE POWER OUTPUT OF AN ENTIRE STAR!
GNN! SHIELD'S ALREADY FAILING! CAN'T KEEP THIS UP MUCH LONGER!
Ah, THE FABLED BATMAN.
READY TO PIT YOUR SKILLS AGAINST MINE?
FINE BY ME. HOW ABOUT "BULLETS AND BRACELETS"?
I DON'T THINK SO.
PTANG
THUK
BLAST!
THAK
THIS MAGIC BOW MAKES MY AIM FLAWLESS!
SO TAKE A MOMENT AND WEIGH YOUR NEXT MOVE CAREFULLY.

IT WILL MOST LIKELY BE YOUR LAST!

THANKS. LET'S TRY THAT AGAIN!

WHHSCHHHHHH
PTANG
Hmm. YOU'RE RIGHT. YOUR AIM IS FLAWLESS.

UNNH!!
ZAKK
SUPERMAN!
DON'T WORRY ON MY ACCOUNT, LANTERN.
MY BODY IS POWERED BY YELLOW SUNLIGHT...
...AND THIS MAGICAL SUN ENERGY IS GIVING ME A SUPER-CHARGE THANKS TO BATMAN'S TRICK!
MAYBE MAGIC ISN'T SO BAD AFTER ALL!
WHAT DO YOU SAY, YOUR MAJESTY? UP FOR ROUND TWO?!

SWEET HERA! WHAT HAVE I DONE?

YOU MADE A ONE-IN-A-MILLION SHOT.
AS DID I-- TO A NERVE CLUSTER RIGHT ...HERE.
Oh...

THIS WAS OVER BEFORE IT BEGAN!
MY SPEED IS GREATER THAN ANYTHING YOU COULD POSSIBLY IMAGINE!
YEAH?! HOW ABOUT THE SPEED OF LIGHT?!
WHAT?
GUESS NOT.
WHAM
NICE SHOT, GL!
BUT WATCH ME DO TWO FOR THE PRICE OF ONE...
...BY CHANGING THE COURSE OF MIGHTY RIVERS!
THINK SUPES HAS THAT COPYRIGHTED?
SSSS
SPASH
KOFF! KOFF!

WE TRIED THIS IN YOUR ELEMENT, AMAZON...
...NOW LET'S TRY IT IN MINE!
Ah! LET GO!
I DON'T CARE HOW POWERFUL YOU'VE BECOME! AS LONG AS I WEAR THESE WINGS...
SPKOW
I CAN NOT BE DEFEATED! ESPECIALLY NOT BY A--
WHO DARES?!
I DO. A MAN.
A MAN WHO'S SET FOOT ON YOUR ISLAND...
BESTED YOUR AMAZONS...
AND WHO NOW ENDS YOUR DREAMS OF CONQUEST!
NO!
CRASH
THWIP
HIPPOLYTA! DESTROY HIM!

AT ONCE, MY GODDESS!
WAKK
BATMAN, WATCH OUT! SHE'S UNBEATABLE!

REALLY? SO AM I!

BOASTFULL MAN! YOUR ARROGANCE WILL BE YOUR UNDOING!
BETTER TIME THIS JUST RIGHT...
...BECAUSE THIS IS GOING TO--

--HURT!
GRR!!
Ah!
SPLUTCH

BY THE GODS, WHAT A MAN! WHAT A HERO!
NOW, MORE THAN EVER, MY COURSE IS CLEAR!
NO GODDESS OF MINE WOULD HAVE US WAR WITH SOULS SO NOBLE--
--BE THEY MALE OR FEMALE!
SACRILEGE! RELEASE ME AT ONCE!
DIANA! YOU BRING ULTIMATE SHAME UPON US ALL!
I THINK NOT, MOTHER. FOR THIS LASSO OF TRUTH IS MY GIFT FROM THE GODS...
...AND NO REAL GODDESS OF TRUTH NEED FEAR IT!
SO SHOW US YOUR TRUE FORM! SHOW US WHO YOU REALLY ARE!
I...I AM...

ARES, GOD OF WAR!
CURSE YOUR INTERFERENCE! I WAS SO CLOSE TO CREATING THE GREATEST CONFLICT EVER!
NOT JUST BROTHER AGAINST BROTHER, BUT BROTHER AGAINST SISTER!
IT'S OVER, ARES! NOW THAT THE TRUTH IS KNOWN, MY SISTERS ARE FREE FROM YOUR SPELLS!
ARE THEY?
AMAZONS, JOIN ME! TOGETHER WE CAN CRUSH THE TYRANNY OF MAN'S WORLD!

NO! THAT IS NOT OUR WAY.
THIS IS AN ISLAND OF PEACE, WAR GOD. THERE IS NO PLACE FOR YOU HERE!
BELIEVE WHAT YOU WILL, PRINCESS. BUT THERE WILL COME A DAY...

IS IT KOFF OVER?
I SURE HOPE SO, BIG GUY!
COME, SISTERS! WE HAVE MUCH TO ATONE FOR!
AND I CAN THINK OF NO BETTER PLACE TO START...

"...THAN THE MENDING OF OUR 'GUESTS.'"
THANK YOU FOR THE USE OF YOUR "PURPLE RAY." ITS HEALING POWERS ARE AMAZING.
REMIND ME TO PAY YOU A VISIT...

...WHEN MY BACK STARTS ACTING UP.
NO, BATMAN. IF I'VE LEARNED ANYTHING THIS DAY...
...IT'S THAT THE GIFTS OF THE GODS SHOULD NOT BE TAKEN LIGHTLY!

AMEN TO THAT!
SMASH

DAUGHTER, BEFORE YOU LEAVE, KNOW THIS.
IN FOLLOWING YOUR ADVENTURES, IT IS OBVIOUS TO ME WHY ARES CHOSE THIS TIME TO STRIKE.
"IT IS BECAUSE MAN'S WORLD, A WORLD CONSTANTLY AT WAR, NOW HAS A NEW LEAGUE OF CHAMPIONS...
"A LEAGUE WHICH GIVES HOPE AND PROMISES PEACE AND JUSTICE FOR ALL!"
THE
END

JUSTICE LEAGUE UNLIMITED

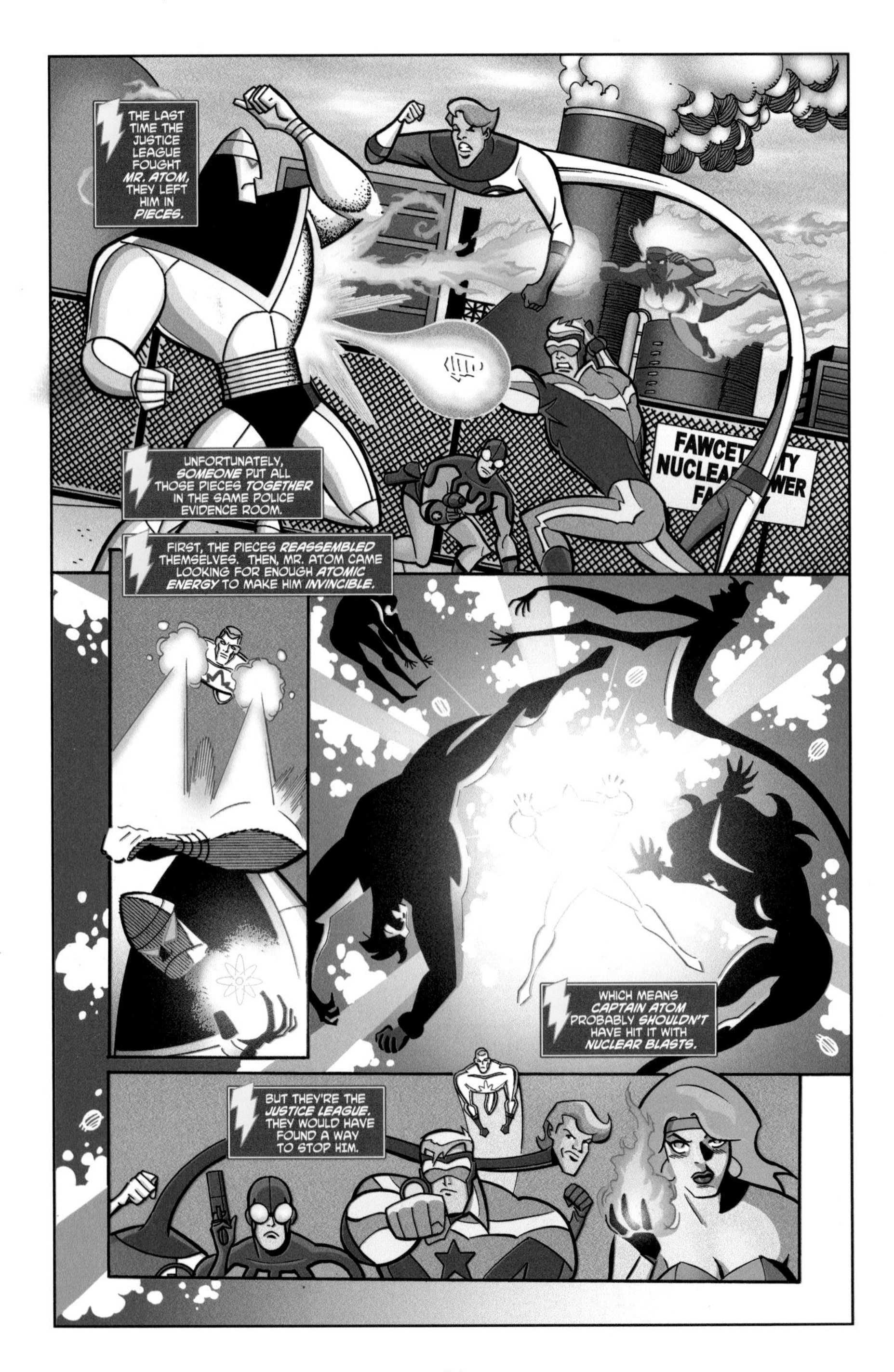
THE LAST TIME THE JUSTICE LEAGUE FOUGHT MR. ATOM, THEY LEFT HIM IN PIECES.
UNFORTUNATELY, SOMEONE PUT ALL THOSE PIECES TOGETHER IN THE SAME POLICE EVIDENCE ROOM.
FIRST, THE PIECES REASSEMBLED THEMSELVES. THEN, MR. ATOM CAME LOOKING FOR ENOUGH ATOMIC ENERGY TO MAKE HIM INVINCIBLE.
WHICH MEANS CAPTAIN ATOM PROBABLY SHOULDN'T HAVE HIT IT WITH NUCLEAR BLASTS.
BUT THEY'RE THE JUSTICE LEAGUE. THEY WOULD HAVE FOUND A WAY TO STOP HIM.

Just Us Girls
PAUL D. STORRIE SCRIPT
RICK BURCHETT ART
HEROIC AGE - COLORS
TRAVIS LANHAM - LETTERS
TY TEMPLETON - COVER ART
MICHAEL WRIGHT - EDITOR
EVEN IF I *DIDN'T* LEND A HAND.
KLANG
NOT TOO LONG AGO, A WIZARD GAVE MY BROTHER, BILLY BATSON, THE POWER TO CHANGE INTO *CAPTAIN MARVEL*, THE WORLD'S MIGHTIEST MORTAL, WITH ONE MAGIC WORD... *SHAZAM!*
TURNS OUT IT WORKS FOR *ME*, TOO.

HEY, KIDDO. THANKS FOR THE ASSIST.
SURE, I...
SO, DO I DETECT A "MARVELOUS" MOTIF TO YOUR OUTFIT?
UM, YES, I...
HOW *IS* THE BIG RED CHEESE?
WHAT? OH. GOOD. HE...
SO, WHAT'S *YOUR* NAME, KIDDO?
MARY... *UH,* I MEAN MARVEL...
MARY MARVEL, HUH? I LIKE IT! WELL, MARY, MEET MY PALS. THAT'S BOOSTER GOLD IN THE GOGGLES AND BLUE BEETLE IN THE OTHER GOGGLES. THE SHINY FELLA IS CAPTAIN ATOM AND THE GORGEOUS GAL IN GREEN IS FIRE.

YOU'LL HAVE TO EXCUSE THE ELONGATED MAN, MARY. SOMETIMES HE'S SO BUSY BEING FRIENDLY THAT HE *FORGETS* MAYBE OTHER PEOPLE HAVE SOMETHING TO SAY.

WELL, I WAS KIND OF HOPING I COULD ASK YOU A FAVOR...

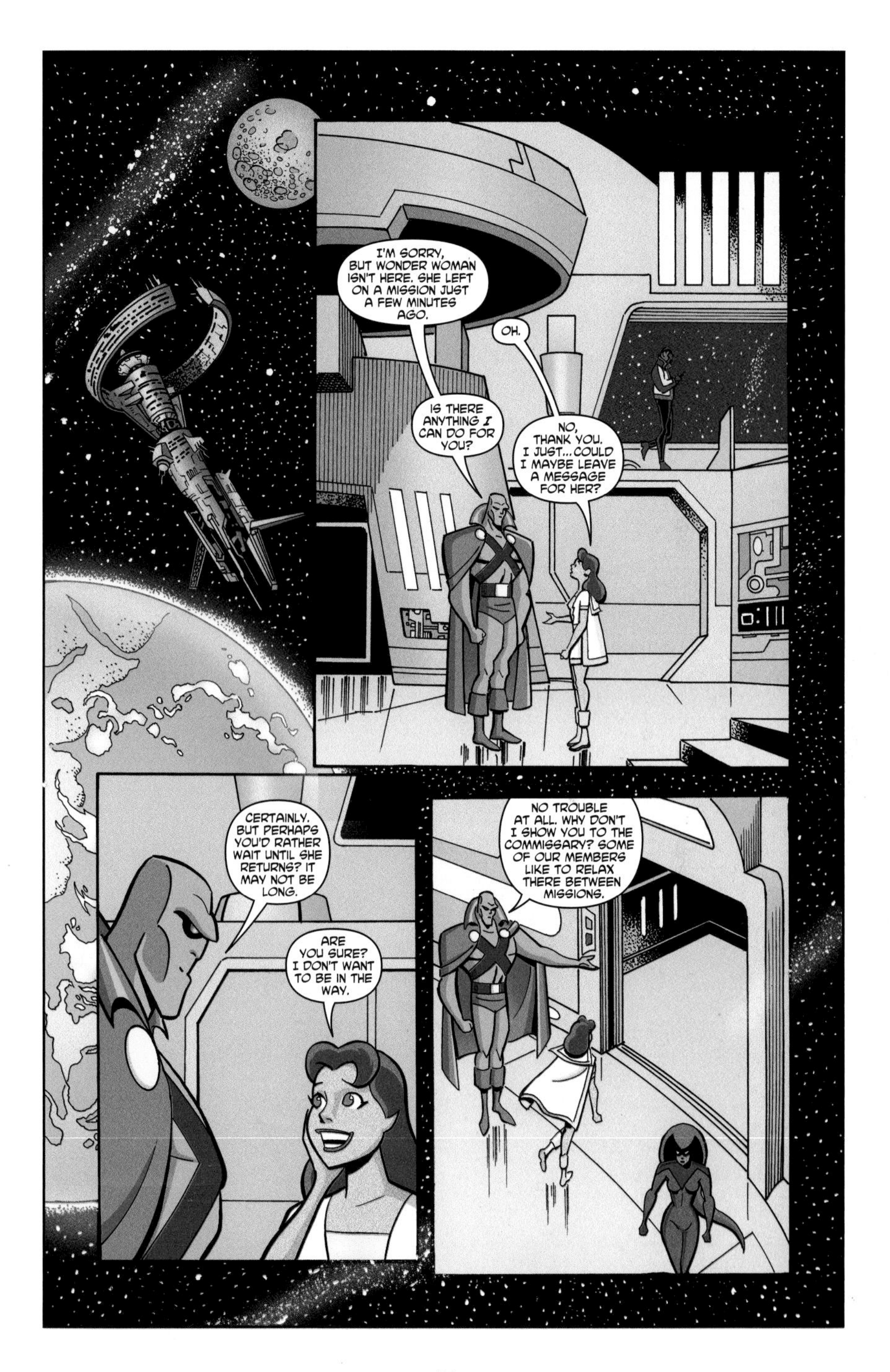
I'M SORRY, BUT WONDER WOMAN ISN'T HERE. SHE LEFT ON A MISSION JUST A FEW MINUTES AGO.
OH.
IS THERE ANYTHING I CAN DO FOR YOU?
NO, THANK YOU. I JUST...COULD I MAYBE LEAVE A MESSAGE FOR HER?
CERTAINLY. BUT PERHAPS YOU'D RATHER WAIT UNTIL SHE RETURNS? IT MAY NOT BE LONG.
ARE YOU SURE? I DON'T WANT TO BE IN THE WAY.
NO TROUBLE AT ALL. WHY DON'T I SHOW YOU TO THE COMMISSARY? SOME OF OUR MEMBERS LIKE TO RELAX THERE BETWEEN MISSIONS.

THIS PLACE IS AMAZING. MY BR... *Er*, CAPTAIN MARVEL TOLD ME A LITTLE, BUT HE DIDN'T DO IT... *Um*... JUSTICE.
PLEASE LET HIM KNOW THAT HE'S WELCOME TO RETURN. HIS DEPARTURE WAS UNDER... UNFORTUNATE CIRCUMSTANCES.
I'LL LET HIM KNOW.
HEY, J'ONN. NEW RECRUIT?
KARA, THIS IS MARY MARVEL. SHE'S WAITING FOR WONDER WOMAN TO RETURN FROM A MISSION. I THOUGHT PERHAPS YOU COULD KEEP HER COMPANY.
SURE THING. GRAB A SEAT.
SO, "MARY MARVEL"?
YEAH. I WAS THINKING OF SOMETHING COOLER, LIKE MARVELLA OR GIRL MARVEL, BUT WHEN ELONGATED MAN ASKED, I KIND OF **SPAZZED.**

DON'T FEEL BAD. SOMETHING LIKE THAT HAPPENED TO BOOSTER GOLD.
I JUST MET HIM. IT SEEMED LIKE A WEIRD NAME. ANY CHANCE I COULD CHANGE MINE NOW?
HA! SORRY, YOU'D BETTER GET USED TO IT. BY NOW, ELONGATED MAN HAS PROBABLY TOLD A HUNDRED PEOPLE. MOST OF THEM REPORTERS.
SO, WHAT DO YOU WANT TO TALK TO WONDER WOMAN ABOUT?
IT'S KIND OF EMBARRASSING, BUT I GUESS YOU'D UNDERSTAND BETTER THAN MOST. I MEAN, YOU'RE SUPERGIRL.
COFFEE

IT'S JUST THAT... WELL, I'M KIND OF JUST THE GIRL VERSION OF CAPTAIN MARVEL. SAME POWERS. SAME EMBLEM. BUT I WANT TO BE MORE THAN THAT.
BELIEVE ME, I CAN RELATE.

I PROBABLY SHOULD HAVE COME LOOKING FOR YOU IN THE FIRST PLACE.
DON'T SWEAT IT. IF I WANTED ADVICE, I'D GO TO DIANA, TOO.
LOOK, THE IMPORTANT THING TO REMEMBER IS...
Y'KNOW WHAT? I'VE GOT A BETTER IDEA THAN BORING YOU WITH A LONG SPEECH.

WH-WHERE ARE WE GOING?
YOU WANTED TO SEE WONDER WOMAN, DIDN'T YOU?

WOW. WHO ARE THESE GUYS?
THEY CALL THEMSELVES THE NEW OLYMPIANS. I READ ABOUT THEM IN THE LEAGUE FILES. USED TO WORK FOR SOME GOTHAM GANGSTER NAMED MAXIE ZEUS.
GRRRRR
WHOOSH
BAH! YOU CANNOT HOPE TO STAND AGAINST MY STRENGTH!
UGH! DO YOU KNOW HOW TIRED I AM OF HEARING THAT?

NEAT TRICK, SHAPESHIFTER. BUT CAN YOU *USE* IT?
AAHHH!
SHAME ON YOU, SPARKY! DON'T YOU KNOW BETTER THAN TO PLAY WITH *FIRE* IN THE WOODS?
OOOF!
GOT YOU, MY LITTLE FIREFLY!
CALL OFF THE HOUNDS, LADY. I'D HATE TO HURT THEM.
WHAT? AREN'T WE GOING TO HELP?
NAW. THEY'RE FINE. JUST WATCH.

"IN CASE YOU'RE WONDERING, THE ONE WITH THE BOW CALLS HERSELF DIANA, LIKE THE ROMAN GODDESS OF THE HUNT. I BET WONDER WOMAN LOVES THAT."
WHY DON'T I SKEWER YOU FOR THEM INSTEAD?
SORRY, PUPS. I TRIED.
A CAREFUL GIRL NEVER LEAVES HOME WITHOUT HER PEPPER SPRAY.
FSSHHH
YIPE
YIPE
YEAH, THEY LOOK JUST LIKE MOMMY.
MY BABIES!
YIPE
YIPE
YIPE

THERE IS A DIFFERENCE BETWEEN WHAT YOU CAN CATCH AND WHAT YOU CAN HOLD!
AIIIEEEE!
"THE HAG IN THE RATTY CAPE IS CALLED NOX, AFTER THE ROMAN GODDESS OF THE NIGHT.
"THE BRUISER IS ANTAEUS. SHARES A NAME WITH SOME GIANT THAT FOUGHT HERCULES."
HA! WITH ALL THIS GOLD, WE CAN LIVE LIKE GODS. DO YOU THINK WE'LL LET YOU STOP US?
YOU CALL YOURSELVES OLYMPIANS, BUT, TRUST ME, YOU'RE NOT EVEN CLOSE!
UNGH!
KLAAAANG
WHAM
ARRRGGH
"THE SHAPESHIFTER'S PROTEUS. MAKES SENSE, IF YOU KNOW YOUR MYTHOLOGY."

HM? YOU'RE RIGHT. THIS LITTLE BIRD IS TOO QUICK FOR ME.
THAT'S RIGHT, PAL. LISTEN TO YOUR IMAGINARY FRIEND.
"THE FLAME THROWER IS VULCANUS. ROMAN GOD OF SMITHS, I THINK. THAT'S WHY THE HAMMER."
AARRRRR
GOOD QUESTION! WHAT *DOES* HAPPEN WHEN SHE'S CUT OFF FROM LIGHT ENTIRELY?
WHA--?!?
BUT WHAT ABOUT *THAT* ONE?
WHY DON'T YOU RUN ALONG, NOX, AND LEND SOMEONE ELSE A HAND?
WHERE DID SHE...?
AH. BEHIND ME.

THOUGHT YOU'D CATCH ME BY SURPRISE?
SLAM
URITY
YOU MONSTER! I'M GOING TO--
CANARY!
NEVER TURN YOUR BACK ON YOUR PREY!
KRAK
I'LL KEEP THAT IN MIND.

WE'D BETTER--
NO, WAIT! SOMETHING STRANGE IS GOING ON.
DUH.
YOU DON'T UNDERSTAND! ONE OF MY POWERS IS *WISDOM.* IT'S TELLING ME THERE'S SOMETHING HAPPENING HERE THAT WE CAN'T SEE.
USE YOUR SUPER SENSES. LOOK AROUND. MAYBE--
GOOD CALL.
BE RIGHT BACK!

MY ADVICE? DON'T GET COCKY.
NO, NO, NO. SOMEONE HELP DIANA. QUICKLY.
GUESS I SHOULD TAKE MY OWN ADVICE.
WHOOSH
YOU'RE ARGUS, RIGHT? FORGOT ABOUT YOU.
DON'T WORRY. I'LL BE GENTLE.
ULP.

ARGHH!
THWAM
FINALLY! THE LIGHT!
ARGUS? WHERE ARE YOU?
NOW THAT MY POWERS HAVE RETURNED, PERHAPS IT'S TIME I PUT THEM TO USE!
ZZAK
AGGHH
NO! THIS CAN'T BE HAPPENING!
WANNA BET?
SSSSHHRRREEEEE

HIII-YA!
NICE FORM.
SORRY IF MINE'S A LITTLE SLOPPY.
WHOOF!
LOOKS LIKE ALL YOUR TEAMMATES HAVE FALLEN. I DON'T SUPPOSE YOU'D CONSIDER SURRENDER?
DIDN'T THINK SO.
THE *REAL* ANTAEUS LOST HIS STRENGTH WHEN HE WASN'T IN CONTACT WITH THE GROUND. HOW ABOUT YOU?
NOOOOOOOOOOO!

SO, WHO'S HE?
ARGUS. HE'S PSYCHIC. MOSTLY CLAIRVOYANT, WITH A LITTLE TELEPATHY. HE WAS HIDING IN THE TREES, WATCHING THE FIGHT IN HIS MIND AND GIVING HIS TEAMMATES ADVICE.
IF IT WEREN'T FOR YOU, THINGS MIGHT HAVE GOTTEN UGLY.
SO, YOU STILL WANNA MEET WONDER WOMAN?
SURE, BUT I DON'T REALLY NEED HER ADVICE ANYMORE. I THINK YOU ALREADY *SHOWED* ME WHAT SHE'S GOING TO *TELL* ME.
OH, YEAH?
SURE. HAWKGIRL, HUNTRESS, DR. LIGHT, BLACK CANARY--WONDER WOMAN CHOSE AN *ENTIRE TEAM* OF GIRLS. AND THEY DID JUST AS WELL AS ANY *GUY* COULD HAVE.
NOT EVEN CLOSE.

FIRST, WONDER WOMAN DIDN'T PICK THE TEAM. J'ONN DID. AND HE PROBABLY DIDN'T EVEN REALIZE THEY WERE ALL FEMALE.
HE'S FROM MARS. THEY WERE ALL SHAPECHANGERS. I DON'T THINK THEY PAID MUCH ATTENTION TO THAT STUFF.
SECOND, J'ONN ALWAYS PICKS TEAMS THE SAME WAY. HE FIGURES OUT WHO'S AVAILABLE AND SENDS THE BEST PEOPLE WITH THE RIGHT POWERS.
"TAKE HUNTRESS--GREEN ARROW IS BETTER WITH HIS BOW, BUT J'ONN SENT HER. WHY?
"MAYBE BECAUSE G.A. GETS A LITTLE CAUGHT UP IN PROVING HE'S THE BEST. ESPECIALLY AGAINST OTHER ARCHERS. HUNTRESS DOESN'T CARE WHO'S BETTER. JUST WHO'S STANDING AT THE END OF THE FIGHT.
"OR DR. LIGHT--GREEN LANTERN CAN DO MOST OF THE SAME STUFF SHE CAN, BUT SHE USES ACTUAL LIGHT AND SHE'S A SCIENTIST. SO SHE CAN USE HER POWERS IN ALL SORTS OF DIFFERENT WAYS.
"OR WONDER WOMAN--THERE ARE A LOT OF PEOPLE IN THE LEAGUE WHO COULD GO TOE-TO-TOE WITH THAT ANTAEUS GOON, BUT SHE KNOWS GREEK MYTHOLOGY BETTER THAN ANYBODY. WANNA BET THAT HELPED?"

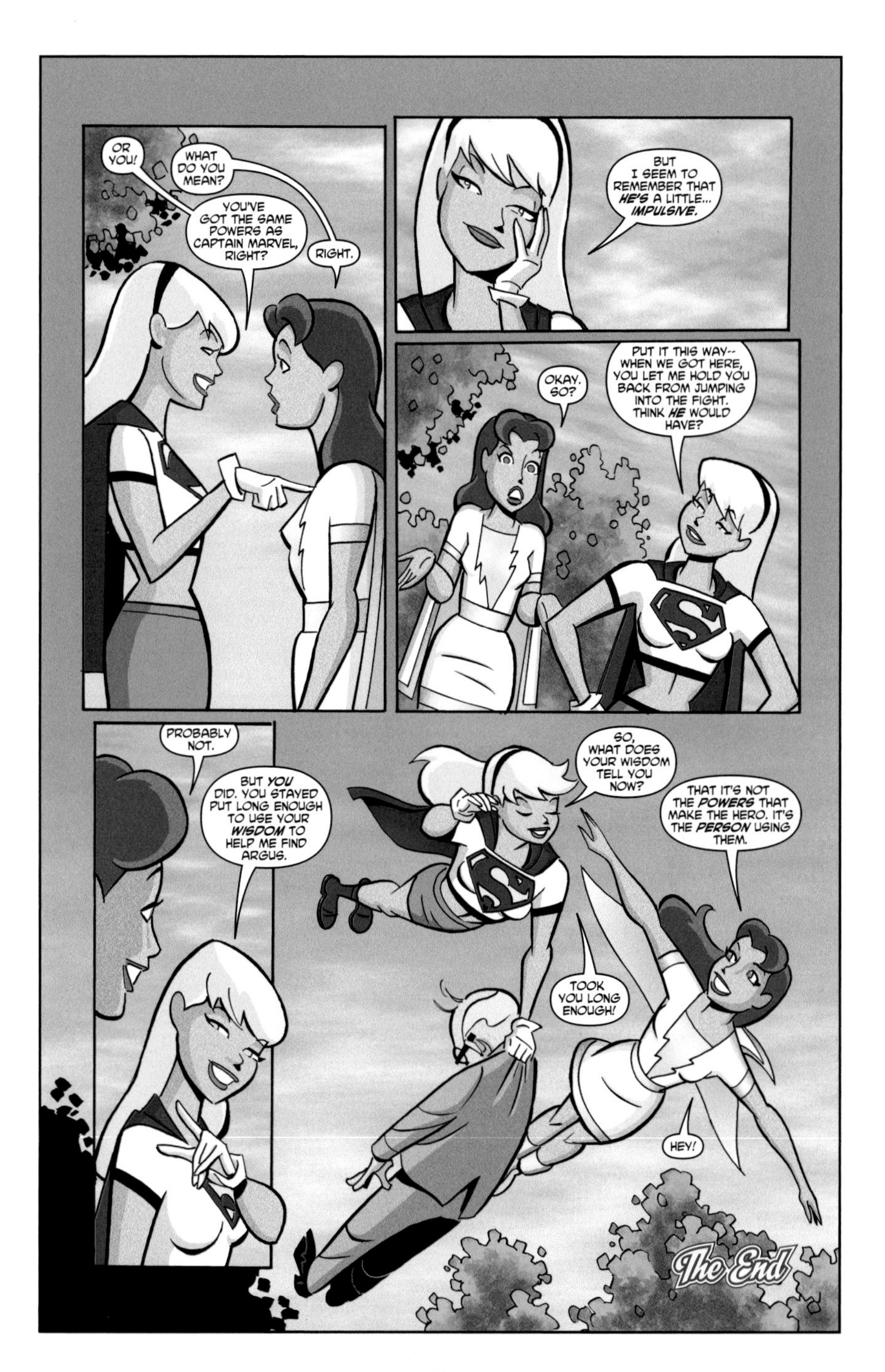
OR YOU!
WHAT DO YOU MEAN?
YOU'VE GOT THE SAME POWERS AS CAPTAIN MARVEL, RIGHT?
RIGHT.
BUT I SEEM TO REMEMBER THAT *HE'S* A LITTLE... *IMPULSIVE.*
OKAY. SO?
PUT IT THIS WAY-- WHEN WE GOT HERE, YOU LET ME HOLD YOU BACK FROM JUMPING INTO THE FIGHT. THINK *HE* WOULD HAVE?
PROBABLY NOT.
BUT *YOU* DID. YOU STAYED PUT LONG ENOUGH TO USE YOUR *WISDOM* TO HELP ME FIND ARGUS.
SO, WHAT DOES YOUR WISDOM TELL YOU NOW?
THAT IT'S NOT THE *POWERS* THAT MAKE THE HERO. IT'S THE *PERSON* USING THEM.
TOOK YOU LONG ENOUGH!
HEY!
The End

JUSTICE LEAGUE UNLIMITED

GYPSIES WANDER. THAT'S THE POPULAR IMAGE OF THEM, HOMELESS PEOPLE WHO MOVE FROM PLACE TO PLACE.
OUTSIDE LOOKING IN
ADAM BEECHEN / SCRIPT
RICK BURCHETT / ART
HEROIC AGE / COLORS
PHIL BALSMAN / LETTERS
TY TEMPLETON / COVER ART
MICHAEL WRIGHT / GYPSY KING
KRAK
WHEN I WAS A KID, THAT'S HOW I FELT--LIKE I DIDN'T BELONG ANYWHERE.
WHOK
TZAAACK
I RAN AWAY FROM HOME, WORE SECOND-HAND CLOTHES, GAINED THE POWER TO TURN INVISIBLE OR BLEND IN AGAINST ANY BACKGROUND...
EVENTUALLY, I WENT BACK TO MY PARENTS, BUT I STILL FELT LIKE I WAS ALONE.
UNTIL I JOINED THE JUSTICE LEAGUE.

SUDDENLY, I FELT LIKE PART OF A FAMILY, SURROUNDED BY PEOPLE WHO HAD MY BACK.
PEOPLE I COULD CALL ON WHEN I NEEDED HELP.
LIKE NOW, FOR EXAMPLE.
THESE WAREHOUSE BURGLARS WOULDN'T BE A PROBLEM, NORMALLY...
...BUT THEY'RE DRESSED LIKE PROS, AND THEY'RE ARMED, AND THERE'S WAY TOO MANY FOR ME TO TAKE ON ALONE, SO I BETTER MAKE LIKE A CHAMELEON...
...AND MAKE THAT CALL.
FIND HER! SHE CAN'T HAVE GONE FAR!
GYPSY TO WATCHTOWER: I NEED IMMEDIATE ASSISTANCE!
I'VE GOT ORGANIZED PARAMILITARY HOSTILES BREAKING INTO A LOCKED WAREHOUSE!
THEY'RE PACKING HIGH-TECH WEAPONS THAT LOOK LIKE THE ONES INTERGANG USED WHEN WE TRASHED THEM LAST MONTH!
UNDERSTOOD, GYPSY.
A MISSION TEAM WILL TELEPORT TO YOUR LOCATION IMMEDIATELY, UNDER CAPTAIN ATOM'S COMMAND.
HOW COME I NEVER GET TO LEAD ANY MISSIONS...?

MY FAMILY'S HERE. THEY CAME BECAUSE I ASKED.
THAT'S A GOOD FEELING.
ALL RIGHT, GYPSY, I'LL TAKE IT FROM HERE...
STANDARD DEPLOYMENT, LEAGUERS...
...HIT 'EM HARD AND FAST!
I THINK CAP LOVES BEING PART OF THE TEAM AS MUCH AS I DO...
...SO LONG AS HE'S THE ONE IN CHARGE.
I DON'T MIND AT ALL.
WHOKK
KLUDD
TIMES LIKE THESE, IT FEELS GOOD TO BLEND IN.

NICE HANDS, ATOM SMASHER!
FZZAPP
NICE SHOT, RAY!
BOK
WHUMP
SPAK
EACH OF US DOES HIS/HER OWN THING.
BUT WE HELP EACH OTHER WHEN WE NEED IT...
MR. TERRIFIC, LOOK OU--NEVER MIND.
SHZZAKK
...JUST LIKE A REAL FAMILY.
CEASE YOUR ATTACK!
WE HAVE A LEGAL DEED TO THIS PROPERTY!
MY KIND OF FIGHT...
...NICE AND QUICK!
ZZOOOOSH

YOU'LL BE HEARING FROM OUR ATTORNEYS FOR THIS ASSAULT!
I'VE NEVER HEARD OF "EPSILON HOLDINGS"...
...BUT THIS PAPERWORK DOES SEEM TO BE IN ORDER.
GYPSY, YOU KNOW THE LEAGUE'S PREPARING FOR THE GLOBAL DEFENSE SUMMIT...
CALLING IN A STRIKE BASED ON YOUR HUNCH JUST DIVERTS US FROM TRULY IMPORTANT BUSINESS!
IF THIS IS SO LEGIT, WHY DO THEY NEED GUNS? WHY SNEAK AROUND IN THE MIDDLE OF THE NIGHT?
WE HAVE PERMITS FOR THE WEAPONS, AND THIS IS A DANGEROUS NEIGHBORHOOD. YOU KNOW...
...PEOPLE CAN GET ATTACKED.

YOU NEED TO GET YOUR FACTS STRAIGHT BEFORE YOU RUSH INTO DECISIONS, GYPSY!
JEEZ, CAP, IT WAS AN HONEST MISTAKE! DON'T--
STAY OUT OF THIS, FLASH.

THE STAKES WE PLAY FOR ARE TOO HIGH FOR ANY MISTAKES!

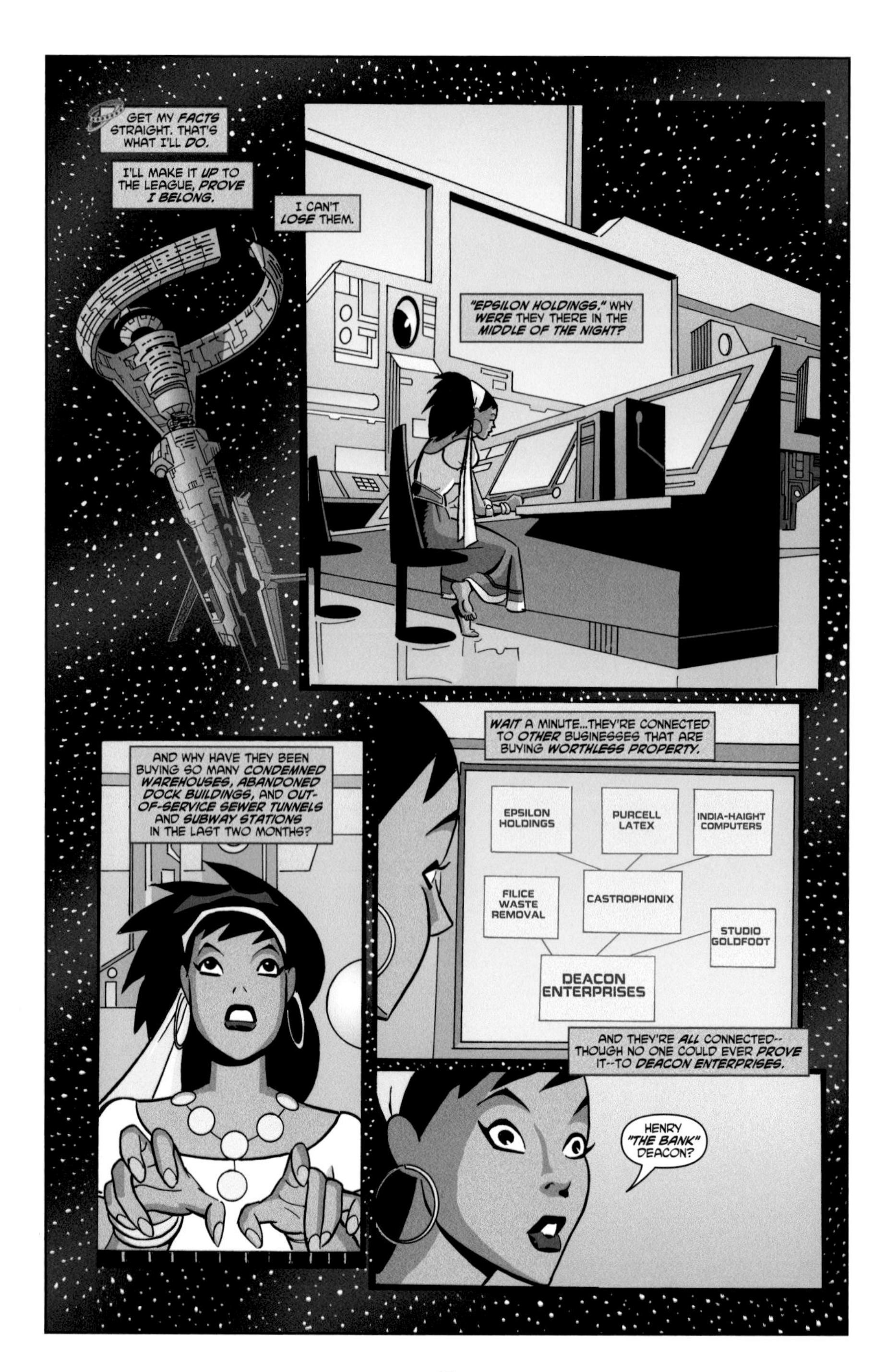
GET MY FACTS STRAIGHT. THAT'S WHAT I'LL DO.
I'LL MAKE IT UP TO THE LEAGUE, PROVE I BELONG.
I CAN'T LOSE THEM.
"EPSILON HOLDINGS." WHY WERE THEY THERE IN THE MIDDLE OF THE NIGHT?
AND WHY HAVE THEY BEEN BUYING SO MANY CONDEMNED WAREHOUSES, ABANDONED DOCK BUILDINGS, AND OUT-OF-SERVICE SEWER TUNNELS AND SUBWAY STATIONS IN THE LAST TWO MONTHS?
WAIT A MINUTE...THEY'RE CONNECTED TO OTHER BUSINESSES THAT ARE BUYING WORTHLESS PROPERTY.
EPSILON HOLDINGS
PURCELL LATEX
INDIA-HAIGHT COMPUTERS
FILICE WASTE REMOVAL
CASTROPHONIX
STUDIO GOLDFOOT
DEACON ENTERPRISES
AND THEY'RE ALL CONNECTED--THOUGH NO ONE COULD EVER PROVE IT--TO DEACON ENTERPRISES.
HENRY "THE BANK" DEACON?

THE RUMOR IS, HE'S PART OF AN ELITE CIRCLE OF BUSINESSMEN...
AROUND THE TOWN
DEACON STEPS OUT
...WHO MAKE THEIR DOUGH BY USING FRONT COMPANIES TO BANKROLL SUPERVILLAINS--LIKE INTERGANG, FOR EXAMPLE.
HIGH-TECH FREAKY PROPS, WEAPONS AND ROBOTS DON'T PAY FOR THEMSELVES, AFTER ALL.
SUPPOSEDLY, DEACON CUTS A DEAL WITH HIS "CLIENTS" FOR A PERCENTAGE OF THEIR TAKE.
IF THEY SCORE BIG, HE SCORES BIG.
IF THEY BLOW IT, HE JUST MOVES ON TO THE NEXT CRIMINAL.
DEACON MAKES SURE THE SUPERVILLAINS DON'T EVEN KNOW WHO'S FUNDING THEM, SO THEY COULDN'T RAT HIM OUT IF THEY WANTED TO.
COMPANIES LIKE EPSILON HOLDINGS TAKE THE FALL.

SO WHAT DOES HE WANT WITH JUNK PROPERTY?
HEY, GYP... JUST WANTED TO SEE HOW YOU WERE DOING...
CAP HIT YOU PRETTY HARD EARLIER...
SOMETIMES HE GETS CARRIED AWAY, THINKS HE'S STILL IN THE SERVICE.
HE WAS RIGHT.
I BLEW IT. I DIDN'T THINK.
YOU'RE TAKING THIS WAY TOO SERIOUSLY!
EVERYONE'S ENTITLED TO GOOF UP ONCE IN A WHILE...
HECK, I'M PRACTICALLY FAMOUS AROUND HERE FOR--
HEY... WHERE DO I KNOW THAT ADDRESS FROM?
624 W. HARDING RD.
1313 MOCKINGBIRD LN.
67 NOEL ST.
72 LIAM ST.
2004 BOOMSTICK GARDENS
102 WONDERWHE
WAIT... THAT'S WHERE THE MIRROR MASTER SET THAT TRAP FOR ME A FEW MONTHS BACK!*
*IT'S TRUE-- CHECK OUT JLU #12!--MW
HE HAD ALL KINDS OF HOLOGRAPHIC GEAR AND WEAPONS IN THERE...

I NEVER THOUGHT ABOUT WHAT HAPPENS TO OLD SUPERVILLAIN HIDEOUTS...
EPSILON
EPSILON HOLDINGS
SOME OF THEM ARE NEVER FOUND, I GUESS.
THEY JUST STAY INTACT, FORGOTTEN...
EPSILON HOLDINGS
THAT'S A LOT OF BAD GUY TECH FLOATING AROUND OUT THERE...
...AND A GUY LIKE DEACON WOULD KNOW WHERE ALL OF IT IS.

WAREHOUSES, DOCKS, TRAIN STATIONS AND SEWERS...ALL TYPICAL SUPERVILLAIN HIDEOUTS.
AND WHAT KIND OF PROPERTY HAS DEACON BEEN BUYING?
OKAY...ANOTHER OLD HIDEOUT BEING PACKED UP BY EPSILON.
STILL, THIS DOESN'T PROVE ANYTHING.
EPSILON
GOTTA MAKE ABSOLUTELY SURE BEFORE I CALL IN THE LEAGUE.
HUH? LOOKS LIKE AN INVENTORY.
MUST BE FOR THE STUFF IN ALL THE HIDEOUTS...BUT WHY'S SOME OF IT NOTED WITH "I.U.P."?
SILON
"I.U.P." WHAT DOES THAT STAND FOR? FEEL LIKE I SHOULD KNOW--
--OH, NO.
THIS IS PRIVATE PROPERTY.
YOU'RE TRESPASSING.

SORRY, GUYS...
...I PROMISE YOU WON'T SEE ME AROUND HERE ANYMORE!
THAT'S WHAT YOU THINK, LADY!
THEY WERE READY FOR ME-- PREPARED FOR MY INVISIBILITY!
EPSILON
VZZH
EPSILON
VZZH
WHOK
WHAK
EPSILON
STILL DON'T HAVE A LEGAL LEG TO STAND ON--I DID BREAK IN...

...BUT I KNOW ENOUGH ABOUT WHAT THESE CREEPS ARE UP TO...

...TO MERIT A CALL TO THE CAVALRY!
GYPSY TO JUSTICE LEAGUE!
I AM AT THE OLD CAMMONS LAKE SUBWAY STATION, NOW OWNED BY EPSILON HOLDINGS!
WHAT?! GYPSY, WE ARE NOT LEAVING THE GLOBAL DEFENSE SUMMIT TO BAIL YOU OUT AGAIN!
GET OUT OF THERE NOW!
NO, YOU GET OUT OF THERE! YOU'RE ABOUT TO BE ATTACKED, RIGHT THERE AT THE INTERNATIONAL UNION PLAZA!
GYPSY, WHAT ON EARTH ARE YOU--
KKKKKKKKK
--TALKING ABOUT...?
ZAM
ZAM
ZAM

HO BOY...

CAP? CAPTAIN ATOM, COME IN!
THE ATTACK'S STARTED.
DEACON'S MEN FOUND A WAY TO ACTIVATE THE TECH HE'S FOUND AND SEND IT AGAINST THE LEAGUE...
THAT MEANS HIS MEN ARE CONTROLLING THEM FROM SOMEWHERE... BUT WHERE?!
STATION CLOSED
NOT FROM HIS HEADQUARTERS... HE WOULDN'T WANT IT TRACED BACK TO HIM.
LOANS
OSED
OES
NOTHING I CAN DO BUT RUN DOWN THE LIST OF PROPERTIES HE'S BOUGHT...
...AND HOPE I GET LUCKY!

KOOM
ZAM
EVERYONE... PROTECT THE CIVILIANS AND DIPLOMATS! THEY'RE FIRST PRIORITY!
ZAM
KABOOM
WORK YOUR WAY TOWARDS ME, SO WE CAN ORGANIZE A DEFENSE FORMA-- UNNGH!
ZAM
KEEP THE FAITH, CAP--WE MAY BE DOWN, BUT WE'RE NOT OUT!
UH, I MAY WANT TO REVISE THAT LAST STATEMENT...

SSKKSKKSSK
DAYS LIKE THESE, I REALLY WISH I HAD A "GYPSYMOBILE."
CHECKING ALL THESE HIDEOUTS ON FOOT IS TAKING TOO MUCH TIME.
SPLOOSH
DANGER HIGH VOLTAGE
I BETTER FIND SOMETHING SOON, OR MY TEAMMATES-- HUH? WHAT'S THIS?
HELLO...!
I'M CLEAR... YOU NEED HELP WITH CAPTAIN ATOM?
NAH...I GOT HIM, NO SWEAT...
I COULD USE A LITTLE HELP WITH THE FLASH, IF YOU'RE AVAILABLE...
HEY...DID ANY OF YOU GUYS LEAVE THE DOOR OPEN?

I'VE WORKED UP ENOUGH MOMENTUM...
...SHOULD BE ABLE TO SHRED THIS CAGE LIKE-- EEYARGGH!
FFRAKK
FFRAKK
SOMEBODY COVER FLASH! COME ON, PEOPLE!
WE NEED *WHUFF!* REINFORCEMENTS! *NGH!* WE NEED--
WHAK
WAIT A MINUTE...THEY'RE STOPPING, JUST STANDING THERE...
WHAT'S GOING ON?

STAY ALERT, AND WATCH EACH OTHER'S BACKS...
WHOEVER JUST TOOK OUT CONSOLE B COULD JUST AS EASILY COME AFTER US...
FZZ FZZ

...OR THE OTHER CONSOLES!
FZZAPP

WE MAY BE DOWN TWO CONTROL PANELS, BUT NOW WE KNOW WHERE TO SHOOT!
ZZAM
HHNNNH!

I THOUGHT THAT MIGHT BE YOU, GYPSY...
COULDN'T LEAVE WELL ENOUGH ALONE AFTER THE LAST TIME YOU BLEW IT, HUH?

NO, I SURE COULDN'T.
KA BOOM
WHUMP

GYPSY TO ANY LEAGUER AT I.U.P. WITH AN OPERATIVE COMM...
...YOUR ROBOT ENEMIES ARE NO LONGER A THREAT...
...I'VE TAKEN CARE OF EVERYTHING FROM HERE.
I'LL MEET YOU AT I.U.P. SHORTLY.

DEACON
MR. DEACON, WE HAVE A REPORT COMING IN FROM EPSILON HOLDINGS AT THE GLOBAL DEFENSE SUMMIT...
THEIR LATEST BUSINESS VENTURE APPARENTLY WAS MET WITH SEVERE OPPOSITION AND WAS UNSUCCESSFUL.
THANK YOU, MS. BAILEY, BUT SUCCESS IS A RELATIVE TERM.
THIS WAS ONLY MY FIRST FORAY INTO ACTING AS OTHER THAN A FINANCIER...
I'LL SIMPLY LEARN FROM THIS...
...AND TRY AGAIN.

IT'S CLEAR I OWE YOU AN APOLOGY, GYPSY...
IF I'D TAKEN YOUR INVESTIGATION MORE SERIOUSLY, TRUSTED YOU MORE, RATHER THAN ASSUMING I KNOW WHAT'S BEST IN EVERY SITUATION...
IT'S OKAY TO LEAN ON YOUR TEAM... I UNDERSTAND THAT NOW...
ANYWAY... YOU DID GOOD, GYPSY.

THANK YOU, CAPTAIN.
"YOU DID GOOD, GYPSY?!" THAT'S INCREDIBLE!
THE NICEST THING I'VE EVER HEARD CAPTAIN ATOM SAY IS, "DROP AND GIVE ME TWENTY!"
SO, NOW THAT CAP'S PROVEN NOBODY'S PERFECT...
...DO YOU THINK I CAN TALK J'ONN INTO LETTING ME FINALLY LEAD A MISSION SOMETIME?
I'VE FOUND A HOME. I'VE FOUND A TEAM, A FAMILY THAT I CAN LEAN ON, AND THAT CAN LEAN ON ME.
THEY'RE NOT GOING ANYWHERE, AND NEITHER AM I.
I MAY FEEL LIKE I'M ON THE OUTSIDE LOOKING IN ONCE IN A WHILE, BUT SO DOES EVERYONE.
I'VE FOUND A PLACE WHERE I TRULY BELONG.
THESE DAYS, ONLY IN TERMS OF MY NAME...
...AM I A GYPSY.
END

JUSTICE LEAGUE UNLIMITED

--STOP LOOKING AT ME LIKE THAT, NATASHA. I TOLD YOU BEFORE AND I'M TELLING YOU AGAIN.
DON'T RUSH IT.
BUT I'M SO TIRED OF BEING TOLD THAT I'M "TOO YOUNG"!
IF I AM, THEN WHY DID YOU TAKE ME ALL THE WAY UP HERE, TO THE WATCHTOWER?
AND-- AND WHY HELP ME BUILD A SUIT OF ARMOR THAT INTERACTS WITH METROPOLIS'S FUTURE TECHNOLOGY IF I'M NOT SUPPOSED TO USE IT, UNCLE JOHN?
STARGIRL'S ALREADY A MEMBER... HECK, EVEN THE FLASH WASN'T THAT MUCH OLDER THAN ME WHEN HE JOINED THE JLA RANKS!
HE WAS YOUNG, SURE, BUT BY JOINING THE LEAGUE, HE COMPLETED A CYCLE IN HIS LIFE THAT STARTED WHEN HE WAS JUST A KID.
HE CAN BE THE FASTEST MAN ALIVE, BUT HE DOESN'T RUSH THINGS.
AND YOUR ARMOR... YOU KNOW IT'S NOT A TOY. YOU'RE A SMART GIRL, 'TASHA, A GENIUS -- AND THAT'S WHY I DON'T WANT TO SEE YOU HOTDOGGING YOUR WAY INTO THE JUSTICE LEAGUE.
WITH TIME, I'M SURE YOU'LL GROW INTO A VALUABLE MEMBER, SWEETHEART. YOU ONLY NEED A LITTLE MORE PATIENCE...
NOW, EXCUSE ME, BUT I'M SUPPOSED TO BE ON MONITOR DUTY...

AND THERE HE GOES *AGAIN*.

HE CALLS ME A GENIUS BUT ALWAYS ENDS UP *TALKING DOWN* TO ME. I GUESS IT GOES WITH HIS "HERO OF THE DAY" GIMMICK.
SOME WAY TO PROVE FAMILY TIES MATTER...
IF HE DOESN'T TRUST ME ENOUGH TO HELP ME BE *ENROLLED* WITH THE LEAGUE...
...THEN WHY DID WE SPEND MONTHS WORKING *TOGETHER* ON MY ARMOR?

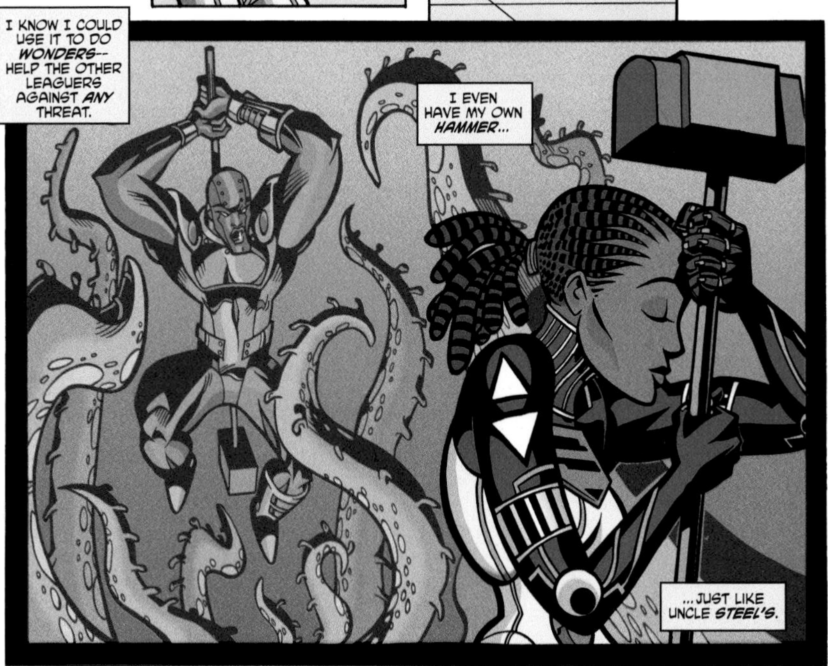
I KNOW I COULD USE IT TO DO *WONDERS*-- HELP THE OTHER LEAGUERS AGAINST *ANY* THREAT.
I EVEN HAVE MY OWN *HAMMER*...
...JUST LIKE UNCLE *STEEL'S*.

BUT IF I'M TO BE, SAY... STEEL *JR.*, THEN WHY ALL THE SLO-MO? WHY NOT TEST MY QUALITIES AND BE *DONE* WITH IT?
IF I'M NOT UP TO THE *TASK*, WELL, WHO CARES -- IT *WON'T*--
OH -- WHO AM I TRYING TO *FOOL*?

I'VE DREAMT OF JOINING THE LEAGUE EVER SINCE I WAS A KID. I WANT TO MAKE A DIFFERENCE... AND I KNOW I CAN.
SAME AS UNCLE JOHN. WHEN HE BECAME STEEL, I WAS SO PROUD OF HIM.

I JUST WISH I COULD HAVE THE CHANCE TO TRY TO MAKE HIM PROUD AS WELL FOR -- HOLD ON A SEC!
WHAT'S THAT?

SKZZT-- THIS IS STEEL CALLING ALL ACTIVE LEAGUERS-- SKZZTT
WE HAVE A SITUATION IN EGYPT WHERE-- AH, STRIKE MY LAST WORDS... IT LOOKS LIKE WE HAVE A DOUBLE TROUBLE NOW, FOLKS!
OH, NO...

...IT'S NOW OR NEVER! UNCLE STEEL CAN'T SAY NO THIS TIME! I CAN HELP! I CAN BE--
--TOO LATE.

IT'S ALREADY ON.
THE LEAGUE IS IN FULL SWING...
...AND ME? I'M STILL STRANDED IN SPACE.
THE CYCLE
MATTEO CASALI-WRITER
SCOTT COHN-PENCILLER
AL NICKERSON-INKER
ROBERT CLARK JR.-LETTERER
HEROIC AGE-COLORIST
RACHEL GLUCKSTERN-EDITOR

SEE IF YOU CAN CONTAIN THE DAMAGE, GREEN LANTERN. I'LL TAKE CARE OF THE BIG GUY.
I'M ON IT, BUT... WAIT--
--MY RING IS PICKING UP SOME WEIRD ENERGY READINGS... STEEL, YOU COPY?

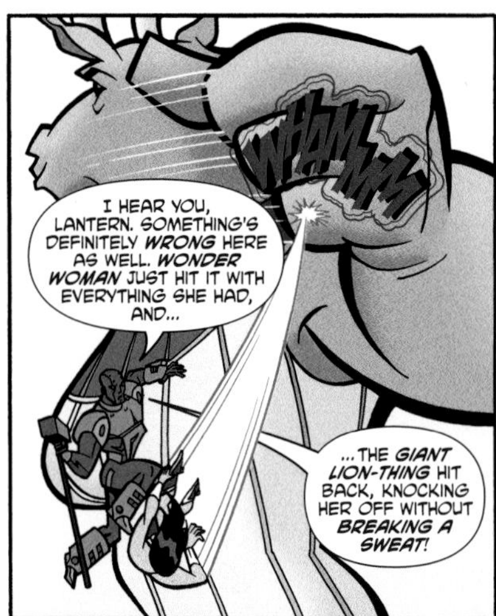
WHAMM
I HEAR YOU, LANTERN. SOMETHING'S DEFINITELY WRONG HERE AS WELL. WONDER WOMAN JUST HIT IT WITH EVERYTHING SHE HAD, AND...
...THE GIANT LION-THING HIT BACK, KNOCKING HER OFF WITHOUT BREAKING A SWEAT!

GREAT RAO! IT'S NOT MAGIC, BUT THIS COLOSSUS IS FUELED BY A FIERCE AND...UNCANNY... ENERGY.
IT'S LIKE FACING AN ELECTROMAGNETIC HURRICANE...I DON'T THINK WE CAN STOP IT LIKE THIS!

LANTERN IS RIGHT. THAT BLOW FELT LIKE I WAS BEING HIT BY THE WHOLE PLANET! THERE MUST BE SOME OTHER WAY...
UNCLE STEEL, CAN YOU HEAR ME?
NATASHA? I'M KINDA BUSY, AT THE MOMENT, SWEETHEART. WHAT IS IT?

I DON'T THINK IT'S OVER YET...

"...NOT BY A LOOOONG SHOT."

NATASHA! STAY WHERE YOU ARE, GIRL, DON'T TRY TO DO ANYTHING-
DON'T WORRY, UNCLE JOHN, EVERYTHING'S COOL. YOU GUYS ALREADY HAVE YOUR HANDS FULL IN EGYPT AND ENGLAND...
...MEXICO'S MINE!
I'LL MAKE YOU PROUD, UNCLE JOHN.
THE WHOLE JUSTICE LEAGUE CAN COUNT ON ME...
NO!
STEEL! WATCH OUT--!
URRGH-!
CLUNNG

SUPERMAN! STEEL IS DOWN AND HIS NIECE, NATASHA, IS OFF ON HER OWN TO FACE A THIRD THREAT!
WE NEED BACK-UP!!
POWER LEVELS AT 37%
WONDER WOMAN'S RIGHT, SUPERMAN. THE GIANT'S TOO STRONG... I CAN'T KEEP THIS UP MUCH LONGER.
AGREED. WE HAVE TO FIND OUT MORE ABOUT OUR OPPONENTS, AND WE NEED SOMEONE TO STOP NATASHA FROM HURTING HERSELF...
...SOMEONE QUICK!
SAY NO MORE, BIG BLUE, I'M ALREADY ON MY WAY TO YUCATAN. WON'T TAKE MORE THAN A COUPLE O' MINUTES...
WELL DONE, FLASH. LANTERN AND I WILL TAKE CARE OF THE PEOPLE HERE AND MEET YOU BACK AT THE WATCHTOWER...
"...WE OBVIOUSLY NEED A BETTER PLAN."
THERE YOU ARE, BIG BOY. IT'S TIME FOR YOU TO LEARN WHAT LITTLE 'TASHA CAN DO!
IF I HAD A HAMMER...
I DON'T KNOW WHY A LAME OLD SONG HELPS ME CONCENTRATE.
BUT IT DOES WORK.

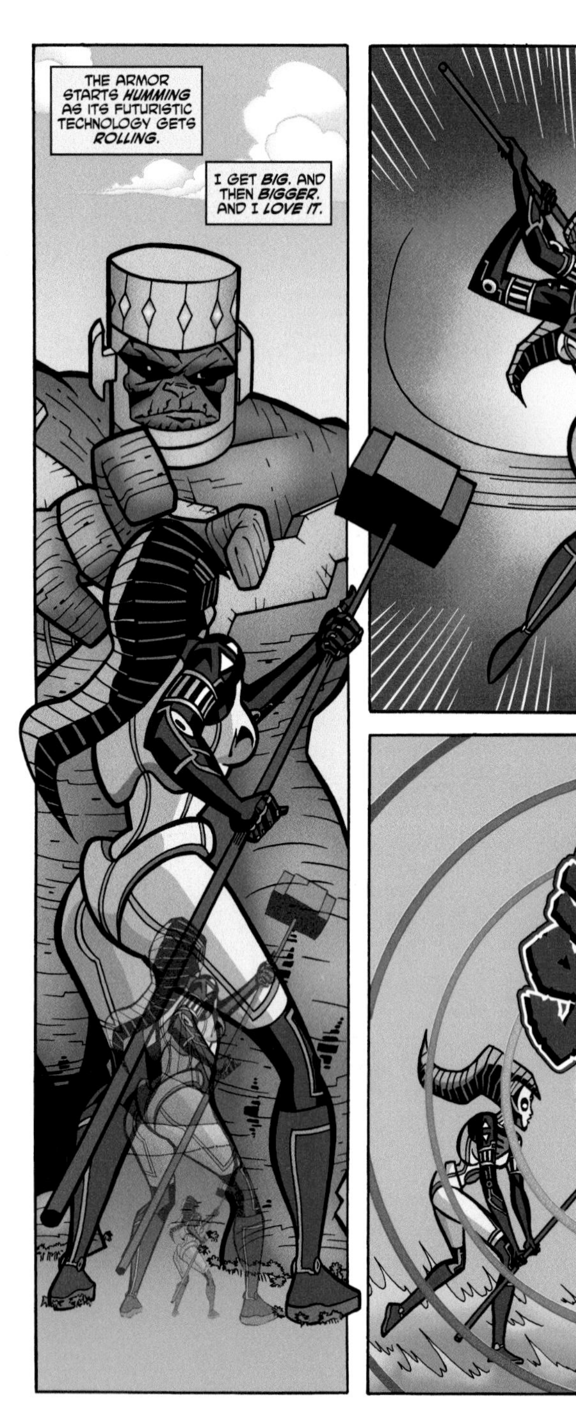
THE ARMOR STARTS HUMMING AS ITS FUTURISTIC TECHNOLOGY GETS ROLLING.
I GET BIG. AND THEN BIGGER. AND I LOVE IT.

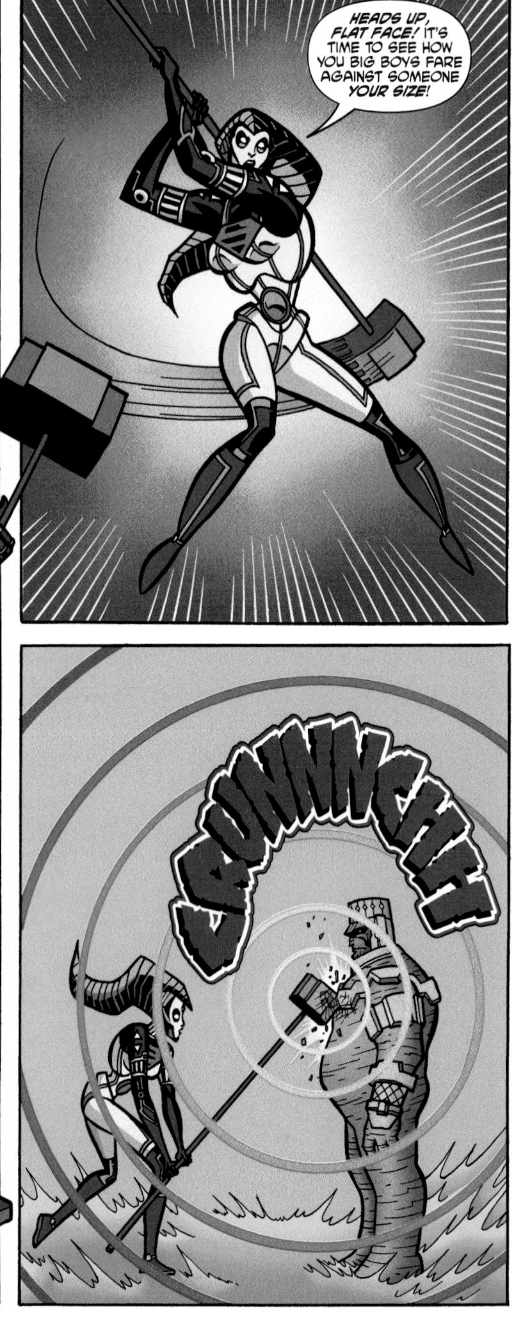
HEADS UP, FLAT FACE! IT'S TIME TO SEE HOW YOU BIG BOYS FARE AGAINST SOMEONE YOUR SIZE!
CRUNNNCHH!

OH, MY--

CRUNCH

N-NO, LET ME GO--

UGH!
K'ROOOM

HE JUST TOSSES ME ASIDE LIKE... LIKE I WAS NOTHING...
AND THE LAST THING I SEE...

...IS THE WAY THE COLOSSUS LOOKS AT ME... WITHOUT RAGE OR HATE, JUST... A KIND OF DISTANT PATIENCE.
THEN JUST A...RED BLUR...
...MOVING... SO FAST...

WHEN I COME TO, FLASH IS THE ONLY ONE SMILING. EVERYBODY ELSE LOOKS SERIOUS.
ESPECIALLY UNCLE STEEL.
--THAT IS WHY YOU CANNOT FIGHT THAT WHICH IS NOT TO BE FOUGHT.
YOU OKAY, KID?

NONSENSE! THE LEAGUE WAS SIMPLY UNPREPARED TO FACE THESE GIANTS. BUT OUR COMBINED POWER IS UNRIVALED!
LET'S TAKE THE FIGHT TO THEM...ONCE MORE!
WHAT-- WHAT'S HAPPENING?
THE LEAGUE HAS CALLED AN EMERGENCY MEETING. DOC FATE IS OFFERING HIS SUGGESTIONS...

"...FROM SOME FARAWAY REALM."
YOUR FIERCE DETERMINATION WON'T BE ENOUGH, HAWKMAN. THEY ARE THE MILLENNIUM GIANTS, SEKHMET, CERNE AND CABRACA.
THEY RISE FROM THEIR SLUMBER TO CLEANSE THE EARTH AND PREPARE FOR ITS NEXT LIFE CYCLE. SO IT HAS BEEN BEFORE. AND SO IT WILL BE AGAIN.

UP TILL NOW, THEY'VE ONLY CAUSED HAVOC AND DESTRUCTION. DO THEY HAVE TO DESTROY A WORLD IN ORDER TO SAVE IT?
THERE MUST BE SOME KIND OF LOGIC TO THEIR ACTIONS--

LOGIC BELONGS TO THE MIND OF MAN. AND THERE IS FAR MORE AT STAKE HERE, BATMAN.
LET'S QUIT THE MUMBO JUMBO TALK, DOC. THOSE THINGS ARE CARVING UP THE LAND LIKE GIANT PLOWS!
HOW DO WE GET BEHIND THE MULE AND STOP 'EM?

HOLD IT RIGHT THERE... THE "LOGIC OF THE PLOW" JUST MIGHT BE IT...
THINK, NATASHA...
REMEMBER THE WAY THE GIANT LOOKED AT YOU...
THAT -- THAT PATIENCE IN HIS GAZE--

YES! YES! I'VE GOT IT! I KNOW HOW TO STOP THE GIANTS!
DON'T YOU THINK YOU'VE ALREADY CAUSED ENOUGH TROUBLE FOR ONE DAY, NATASHA--?

LET HER SPEAK, STEEL. WE ALL KNOW NATASHA IS A SMART GIRL. AND SHE'S ALREADY PROVED HER BRAVERY... LET'S HEAR WHAT SHE HAS TO SAY.
WOW... T-THANKS, WONDER WOMAN...

IT'S -- THE CYCLE DOCTOR FATE WAS TALKING ABOUT IS THE KEY. JUST LIKE YOU ALWAYS SAY, UNCLE STEEL!
THESE COLOSSI ARE HERE TO COMPLETE ONE AND GIVE BIRTH TO THE NEXT. THEY REALLY MEAN NO HARM...THEY ARE PART OF THE PLANET'S LIFE CYCLE!

THAT WOULD EXPLAIN THE ENERGY THAT FUELS THEM.
AND THAT'S WHY WONDER WOMAN FELT LIKE THE WHOLE PLANET WAS HITTING HER!

THE LEY LINES... THE ELECTROMAGNETIC GRID THAT COVERS THE EARTH... THEY FOLLOW IT LIKE A PATH.
SEE, I WAS RIGHT... THEY ARE THE PLOW AND THE MULE!

EXACTLY! AND I KNOW JUST HOW TO CLEANSE THOSE LEY LINES IN A QUICKER AND LESS MESSY WAY THAN THE GIANTS ARE DOING.
TRYING TO PUNCH SOME SENSE INTO THEM WAS POINTLESS. I TRIED TO DO IT 'CAUSE IT'S... WELL, IT'S WHAT YOU GUYS IN THE LEAGUE ALWAYS DO, RIGHT?

UHMM-- RIGHT...
TELL US WHAT YOU HAVE IN MIND, NATASHA.

I WILL NEED TO REPAIR AND RECONFIGURE MY HAMMER. I KNOW I CAN...
...BUT ONLY IF UNCLE STEEL HELPS ME...

HRMM--
C'MON, GIVE HER A BREAK, MAN. IF YOUR NIECE'S RIGHT -- AND SOMETHING TELLS ME SHE JUST MIGHT BE -- WE'LL TUCK THOSE BIG BOYS BACK INTO BED!

OKAY. LET'S GET DOWN AND DO IT.

I CAN'T BELIEVE IT! UNCLE JOHN AND I -- WORKING TOGETHER AGAIN!
AND THIS TIME IT'S FOR THE JUSTICE LEAGUE!

THE NEXT SEVEN HOURS ARE FILLED WITH FRANTIC ACTIVITY AND TEAMWORK. EVERYBODY FOLLOWS MY DIRECTIONS AND HELPS ME ALTER THE HAMMER'S STRUCTURE.

UNCLE JOHN'S EXPERIENCE IS PRICELESS. WITHOUT HIM, NONE OF THIS WOULD BE POSSIBLE.

WE HAVE NO TIME TO LOSE. THE LEAGUE CLEARS THE WAY FOR THE MILLENNIUM GIANTS, BUT EVENTUALLY THEY WILL RUN INTO A MAJOR CITY.
WE CAN'T ALLOW THAT TO HAPPEN. EVERYBODY STRETCHES HIM -- AND HERSELF TO THE LIMIT.
-- YOU GUYS READY? I'M TIRED OF JUST KEEPIN' AN EYE ON THIS MONSTER... AND NOT HAVING HIM TASTE MY MACE!
DON'T WORRY, HAWKMAN --
-- WE'RE ALREADY ON OUR WAY.
ARE YOU SURE THE MODIFIED HAMMER WILL BE ABLE TO HURT CABRACA, SWEETHEART?
NO, UNCLE STEEL...

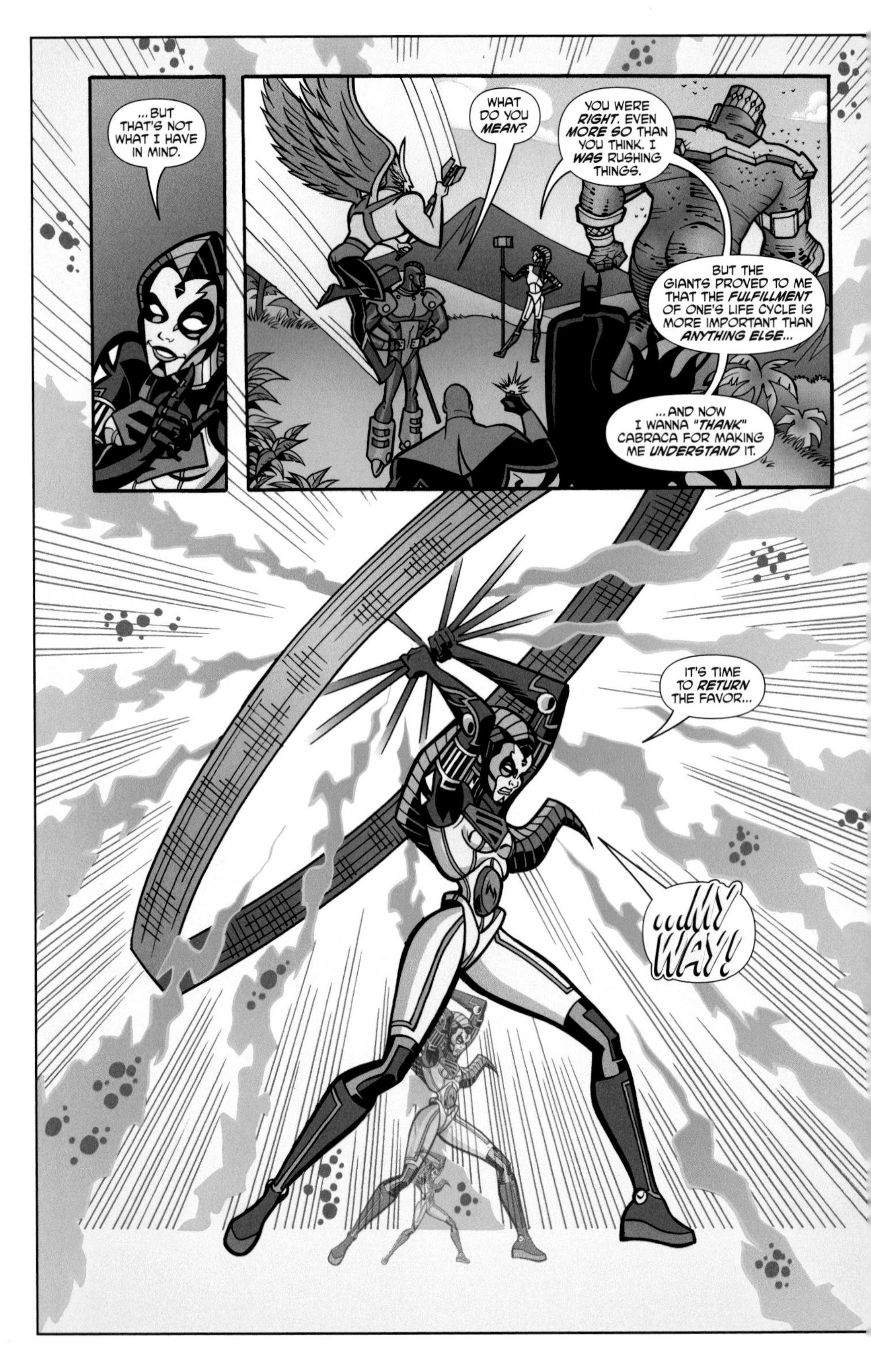
...BUT THAT'S NOT WHAT I HAVE IN MIND.
WHAT DO YOU MEAN?
YOU WERE RIGHT. EVEN MORE SO THAN YOU THINK. I WAS RUSHING THINGS.
BUT THE GIANTS PROVED TO ME THAT THE FULFILLMENT OF ONE'S LIFE CYCLE IS MORE IMPORTANT THAN ANYTHING ELSE...
...AND NOW I WANNA "THANK" CABRACA FOR MAKING ME UNDERSTAND IT.
IT'S TIME TO RETURN THE FAVOR...
...MY WAY!

DESPITE THE BRUTAL ENERGY BACKLASH, I MANAGE NOT TO PASS OUT.
GREAT RA!
YEAH! WAY TO GO, GIRL!
AND I'M ABLE TO SEE MY PLAN IS WORKING... THE ENERGY THAT WAS STORED IN MY HAMMER FLOWS ALONG THE LEY LINES GRID...

...ALL THE WAY TO ENGLAND...
--AND THE FAT BIRD IS SINKING, NOW!
TELL STEEL THE GIRL WAS AB-SO-LUTELY RIGHT!

...DOWN TO EGYPT.
--SEKHMET IS DOWN AS WELL. LOOKS LIKE WE DID IT, GUYS.
IT LOOKS LIKE WE OWE NATASHA ONE.

I WATCH THE COLOSSUS SINK BACK INTO HIS MILLENNIUM-LONG SLUMBER AND CAN'T HELP FEELING A BIT SORRY FOR HIM.
HIS CYCLE HAS BEEN FULFILLED AND IT'S TIME FOR HIM TO MOVE ON TO THE NEXT PHASE.

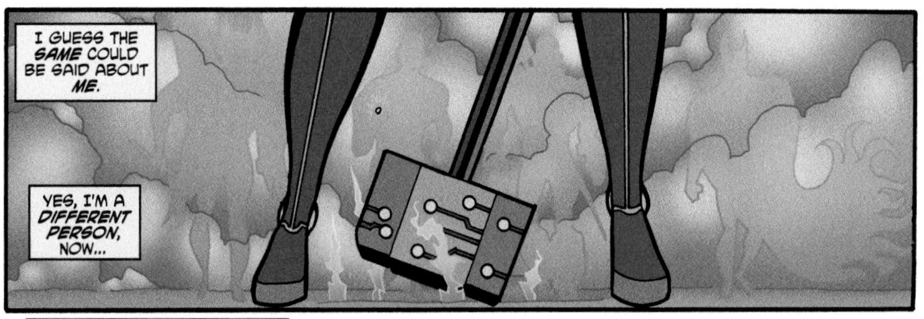
I GUESS THE SAME COULD BE SAID ABOUT ME.
YES, I'M A DIFFERENT PERSON, NOW...

...AND I WILL REMEMBER CABRACA'S SILENT GAZE ALL MY LIFE.
WITHOUT KNOWING IT, HE SHOWED ME THE PATH I WAS SUPPOSED TO FOLLOW FROM THE VERY BEGINNING...ONE OF PATIENCE.

I KNOW THAT, NOW. AND EVEN IF THE JUSTICE LEAGUE MIGHT NOW TREAT ME LIKE A WARRIOR... LIKE ONE OF THEM...
...I KNOW I'M MY OWN GIRL AND I NO LONGER FEEL THE NEED TO EMULATE OTHER HEROES.

AND JUST LIKE UNCLE STEEL SAID...
...WITH TIME, I'LL FIND MY OWN PLACE IN THIS CRAZY OLD WORLD.
THE END

JUSTICE LEAGUE UNLIMITED

HAS IT BEEN THREE YEARS ALREADY? WELL, CONGRATULATIONS, QUEEN.
DON'T CALL ME THAT. MY NAME IS UNA. UNA HITCHENS.
AH, YOU'LL ALWAYS BE QUEEN TO ME. HERE'S EVERYTHING YOU HAD ON YOU WHEN THEY THREW YOU IN HERE.
PROPERTY DEP
STAND BEHIND YELLOW LINE

KEYS. A WRISTWATCH. A HAIRBRUSH. A WALLET WITH $52 CASH.
AND A DECK OF PLAYING CARDS. FUNNY-- WHY TAKE AWAY YOUR COSTUME IF THEY'RE GOING TO LET YOU KEEP YOUR CRIME GEAR?
I TOLD YOU. I'M NOT QUEEN ANYMORE. THOSE ARE JUST CARDS.

IT'S GOOD TO HEAR YOU SAY THAT OUT LOUD.
GASP WONDER WOMAN! WHAT ARE YOU DOING HERE?
I'M HERE TO SHOW YOU THAT I CARE ABOUT YOU, UNA. THIS MUST BE A SCARY TIME, BUT I KNOW YOU CAN STAY STRAIGHT IF YOU TRY.

I CAN'T FIGURE IT OUT-- I JUST DON'T FEEL LIKE I'M WORTH YOUR TROUBLE.
AN IMPORTANT HERO LIKE YOU.
OF COURSE YOU'RE WORTH IT, UNA! YOU'VE PROVEN YOU CAN RISE ABOVE YOUR CRIMINAL TENDENCIES-- THAT YOU CAN FIT IN WITH SOCIETY AND PUT OTHERS' INTERESTS BEFORE YOUR OWN.

YOU HAVE A HUGE CHANCE TODAY. IT'S A CHANCE TO TURN YOUR BACK ON CRIME FOREVER.
I KNOW. I ONLY HOPE IT'S NOT TOO LATE FOR ME, WONDER WOMAN.
I DON'T WANT TO BE A MARKED CARD.

RAW DEAL
DAN RASPLER -Writer
CHRISTOPHER JONES -Penciller
MARK PROPST -Inker
SAL CIPRIANO -Letterer
HEROIC AGE -Colorist
RACHEL GLUCKSTERN & STEVE WACKER -Editors
HOME AGAIN, HOME AGAIN.
BOY, THE OLD NEIGHBORHOOD HASN'T CHANGED TOO MUCH. IT'S STILL GOOD OL' SUICIDE SLUM.
MAYBE SHE'S RIGHT. SHE IS WONDER WOMAN, AFTER ALL.
MAYBE I CAN MAKE SOMETHING OF MY LIFE.
MAYBE I SHOULD LOOK UP SOME OLD FRIENDS. I JUST HOPE I DON'T RUN INTO–
QUEENIE!
--THE GANG.
HEY, HEY! YOU DON'T THINK WE'D MISS YOUR BIG HOMECOMING!
WELCOME HOME, BEAUTIFUL!
HEY, GIVE US A HUG, KID!
NOW, BOYS, DON'T CROWD HER. SHE'S NOT SUPPOSED TO BE SEEN HANGING OUT WITH US, REMEMBER?
THANKS, KING-- I MEAN, HENRY. THANKS. I REALLY SHOULDN'T.
EXACTLY. SO WHY DON'T WE STEP IN HERE REAL QUICK, JUST SO WE CAN WELCOME YOU HOME PROPER?

GEE, THANKS FOR THIS, GUYS. IT'S GOOD TO KNOW YOU DIDN'T FORGET ABOUT ME!
ARE YOU KIDDIN'? WE TOASTED YOU IN HERE ALL THE TIME!
GET OUTTA HERE!
SERIOUSLY!
MENS
HEY, YA KNOW WHO I BUMPED INTO LAST WEEK? CHIPS FUNKLE-- THE JOKER'S OLD HENCHMAN.
SORT OF, YEAH. HE SAYS HELLO.
YEAH? HE EVER GET HIS SIGHT BACK?
OH, HEY, JACK-- I MEAN, CHESTER. YOUR DAD EVER GET THE RESULTS OF THAT HEALTH EXAM?
YEAH, YEAH. HE'S DOING GREAT! DOC SAYS HE CAN GO BACK TO WORK MONDAY.
THANK GOODNESS!
YEAH, WHAT A RELIEF, HUH?
ERNIE, CAN WE GET ANOTHER ROUND HERE? IN FACT...YA KNOW WHAT?
I'M BUYING A ROUND FOR THE HOUSE! IT'S NOT EVERY DAY MY BEST FRIEND GETS OUT OF JAIL!
YOU GOT IT, KING.
HENRY, YOU DON'T HAVE TO DO THAT!
HEY, DID...DID YOU JUST CALL ME YOUR BEST FRIEND?
SURE DID! I MISSED YOU SOMETHING TERRIBLE, KID. WE ALL DID.
OH, YOU GUYS. OH MAN.
I MISSED YOU, TOO.

LATER...
I LOVE THIS PLACE, YOU KNOW WHY? NONE OF THOSE TERRIBLE COMPUTER GAMES. ONLY GAMES YA SEE IN HERE ARE THE REAL ONES, LIKE POKER AND BLACKJACK. REAL GAMES YOU PLAY WITH REAL PEOPLE.
JAIL WAS LIKE THAT, TOO.
HA! DID YOU PLAY A LOT WHEN YOU WERE INSIDE?

SURE, ALL THE TIME. STILL CAN'T BLUFF. BUT I LEARNED SOME NEW GAMES. WE PLAYED FOR FUN, MOSTLY.
I JUST LOVE PLAYING CARDS, THAT'S ALL.
HEY, I DON'T HAVE TO TELL YOU GUYS THAT, RIGHT?
'COURSE YOU DON'T. I'M GLAD TO HEAR YOU STILL FEEL THAT WAY.
QUEEN.

UNA.
LISTEN... THERE'S A JOB...
NOT INTERESTED, HENRY.
KING.

A REAL ESTATE DEVELOPER NAMED FOX STRICKLAND WANTS TO PAY US 20 GRAND TO TORCH-- GET THIS! --A VIDEO ARCADE HE OWNS. WITH THE INSURANCE MONEY, HE WANTS TO BUILD-- READY?-- A CASINO!
HENRY. FORGET IT.
A CASINO, UNA. WITH REAL CARDS AND REAL PEOPLE INSTEAD OF THAT COMPUTERIZED HOGWASH.
AND WE WOULD GET TO DO IT, NOT THAT POSEUR TEAM THE GOVERNMENT NAMED AFTER US. WE'D SHOW THEM WHO THE REAL DEAL IS.
SEE? IT'S PERFECT FOR US! WHADDAYA SAY?

I TOLD YOU, HENRY. DEAL ME OUT.

WHAT ARE--
WAIT.
WELL, THAT DIDN'T WORK! I TOLD YOU WE SHOULDN'T HIT HER WITH THIS ON HER FIRST DAY OUT!
WE'VE GOT A DEADLINE, JACK! I THOUGHT SHE WAS COMING AROUND.
THEY GOT TO HER IN THERE, KING. THE HEADSHRINKERS RESHUFFLED HER SOMEHOW.
NAH. NOT HER. NOT THE QUEEN.
THEY MIGHT HAVE CONFUSED HER FOR A FEW HANDS, BUT THEY DIDN'T BREAK HER.
SHE SAID IT HERSELF-- SHE PLAYED CARDS THE WHOLE TIME SHE WAS IN JAIL. SHE'S STILL ONE OF US!
YOU SEE HER EYES WHEN I DESCRIBED THE JOB? WRECKING A VIDEO ARCADE TO BUILD A CARD PALACE? SHE HAD THE FIRE, I TELL YOU! SHE STILL HAD IT!
KING'S RIGHT. I SAW IT. WE ALL DID.
I DON'T KNOW, GUYS...
WELL, I DO. AND I'M TELLING YOU, IT'S NOT OVER YET.
SHE'S TEETERING ON THE EDGE. SHE'S JUST TIRED. LET HER THINK ABOUT IT FOR A DAY, THEN WE'LL TRY AGAIN.
TRUST ME.
SHE'LL FOLD.

THIRTEEN DOLLARS, PLEASE.
IT'S FOR A *GOOD* CAUSE.
I *GUESS* SO.

OH, BUT IT IS! THE SUICIDE SLUM DEVELOPMENT ASSOCIATION IS RAISING MONEY TO *BUY* THIS LAND FROM A LOCAL DEVELOPER! WE HOPE TO PUT UP A *COMMUNITY CENTER* HERE, NEXT TO THE VIDEO ARCADE.
THANKS! I GUESS IT *IS* A GOOD CAUSE. SURE WOULD BEAT HAVING MY KIDS RUN AROUND THESE DANGEROUS SLUMS AFTER SCHOOL!

KEEP IT UP, UNA! YOU'RE REALLY *SELLING* THEM ON THIS!
BUT IT'S TRUE! IT *IS* A GOOD CAUSE!
I KNOW IT IS. BUT IT'S OBVIOUS YOU FEEL *STRONGLY* ABOUT IT, AND PEOPLE CAN SEE THAT. IT'S SO GREAT TO HAVE YOU *VOLUNTEER.*
CASH BOX
THANKS FOR *LETTING* ME. I KNOW YOU PROBABLY TOOK SOME HEAT FOR ME.
NOT AT ALL...
...WELL, A LITTLE. I MEAN, YOU WERE A *SUPER-VILLAIN* AND ALL. AND YOU DID FIGHT THE *JUSTICE LEAGUE.*
BUT THOSE DAYS ARE OVER, RIGHT?
COMMUNITY

ALTHOUGH I ADMIT WE DID HAVE A LITTLE... INSURANCE.
JUST IN CASE.
GREEN LANTERN-- HERE?
AND WONDER WOMAN, TOO. SHE'S WANDERING AROUND, SHAKING HANDS AND KISSING BABIES. IT'S GREAT OF THE JUSTICE LEAGUE TO PITCH IN WHEN IT'S JUST COMMUNITY FOLKS LOOKING FOR A LITTLE HELP.
I-- I GUESS.
UNA?
NO, NO, OF COURSE IT IS. IT'S A GREAT THING TO HAVE THEM HERE.
GREAT ROLE MODELS FOR THE KIDS, RIGHT? TEACH THEM FROM THE START WHAT IT MEANS TO HELP OTHERS.

I'M SORRY, LOUISE. DIDN'T MEAN TO WORRY YOU THERE. THOSE TWO HEROES ARE GOOD PEOPLE, AND IT'S JUST FEAR... AND SHAME... THAT MAKES THEM SCARY TO ME.
BECAUSE BELIEVE ME-- IF YOU'RE A SUPER-VILLAIN? THOSE ARE TWO VERY SCARY PEOPLE TO HAVE CHASING YOU!
HEH! I GUESS SO!

TRUST ME! THESE DAYS? THESE DAYS, I KNOW THEY'D NEVER DO ANYTHING TO HURT ME.

THIS WOMAN GIVING YOU ANY TROUBLE, MISS?

W-WHAT? NO. NO, OF COURSE--
LOUISE? I'M RIGHT HERE. IF THE QUEEN HAS THREATENED YOU IN ANY WAY, I CAN MAKE SURE SHE--
NO! NOT AT ALL!
OH.

MM-HM.
YOU'RE A GOOD PERSON, LOUISE. ORGANIZING THIS PROJECT. ALLOWING FELONS LIKE THE QUEEN HERE TO MINGLE WITH PROPER CITIZENS.
PLEASE, GREEN LANTERN. UNA HAS VOLUNTEERED A LOT OF TIME AND ENERGY TO--
I SEE SHE'S ARRANGED TO MANAGE THE CASH BOX FOR YOU. VERY NOBLE OF HER.

GREEN LANTERN? WHAT IS-- UNA? I DIDN'T KNOW YOU WERE HERE.
I'M NOT. I'M JUST GOING.
THANKS, LOUISE. FOR EVERYTHING.

WHAT WAS THAT ALL ABOUT? WHAT DID YOU SAY TO THAT POOR WOMAN?
JUST CHECKING UP ON A KNOWN SUPER-FELON, DIANA.
YOU'RE TREATING HER LIKE A SUSPECT-- ROBBING HER OF HER DIGNITY!

WELL, I'D RATHER HAVE SOMEONE ROB ME OF MY DIGNITY THAN MY LIFE SAVINGS!
OH, YOU WOULD? WELL, I'D RATHER IF MY TEAMMATES TREATED THEIR FELLOW HUMAN BEINGS WITH SOME BASIC RESPECT!
HONESTLY, JOHN. JUST TAKE A MOMENT TO THINK OF UNA AS AN "EARTHLING" INSTEAD OF A "FELON," AND YOU'LL SEE WHAT I MEAN.

AND THEN HE LOOKED AT ME LIKE I WAS SOME SORT OF ANIMAL. LIKE I HAD THREE EYES AND GILLS.
WHAT A JERK.
I ALWAYS HATED THAT GUY.
AND IT'S JUST SO FRUSTRATING.
ALL I'M TRYING TO DO IS GIVE SOMETHING BACK TO THIS NEIGHBORHOOD. GOD KNOWS I TOOK ENOUGH OUT OF IT OVER THE YEARS.
THAT VACANT LOT IS A PERFECT PLACE FOR THE NEW COMMUNITY CENTER! AND THE PEOPLE RAISING THE MONEY ARE ALL SO NICE!
THEY'RE SUCH GOOD PEOPLE, HENRY.
WELL, YOU COULD CERTAINLY HELP 'EM TO A COUPLE GRAND, AT LEAST, AN' HAVE PLENTY LEFT OVER TO TREAT YOURSELF TO A LOT OF NICE THINGS!

...
WHAT DO YOU MEAN, ACE?
I'M JUST SAYING, TWENTY GRAND, SPLIT FIVE WAYS AND NO TAXES...WE COULD ALL ANTE UP FOR YOUR CENTER AND STILL LIVE A LITTLE.
...TWENTY GRAND. YOU'RE TALKING ABOUT THAT ARSON JOB.
ACE--!
IDIOT.
WHAT?
IS...IS THAT ALL I MEAN TO YOU GUYS?
SITTING HERE, BEING NICE TO ME-- GIVING ME A SHOULDER TO CRY ON. LETTING ME OPEN UP TO YOU LIKE THIS...!
I TOLD YOU GUYS! HENRY, I TOLD YOU!
NO, QUEEN! YA GOT IT ALL WRONG!
UNA!
MY NAME IS UNA! AND DON'T YOU FORGET IT! EVER AGAIN!
FWOOSH

LATER...
UNA! WHAT ARE YOU DOING?
YAH!
OH, I SEE.
I APOLOGIZE. I THOUGHT YOU...
I-- I WAS HEATING UP A POT OF SOUP!
I AM SORRY. I ASSUMED THE WORST.
WE HAD A REPORT THAT YOU MAY HAVE BEEN CONSORTING WITH SOME *SUSPICIOUS* CHARACTERS EARLIER THIS EVENING, AND I WANTED TO MAKE SURE YOU WERE... ALL RIGHT.

S-SUSPICIOUS? N-NO. NO, I WASN'T CONSORTING WITH ANYONE, WONDER WOMAN. I'VE BEEN...
I'M ALL ALONE, WONDER WOMAN.
UNA, YOU'RE NOT--
WONDER WOMAN, THIS IS GL. WE HAVE A CODE THREE.
HADES...
I HAVE TO GO. BUT I'LL BE BACK. I--
PLEASE!
PLEASE JUST...
WONDER WOMAN, MAKE THAT A CODE TWO!
CAN'T YOU JUST LEAVE ME ALONE?

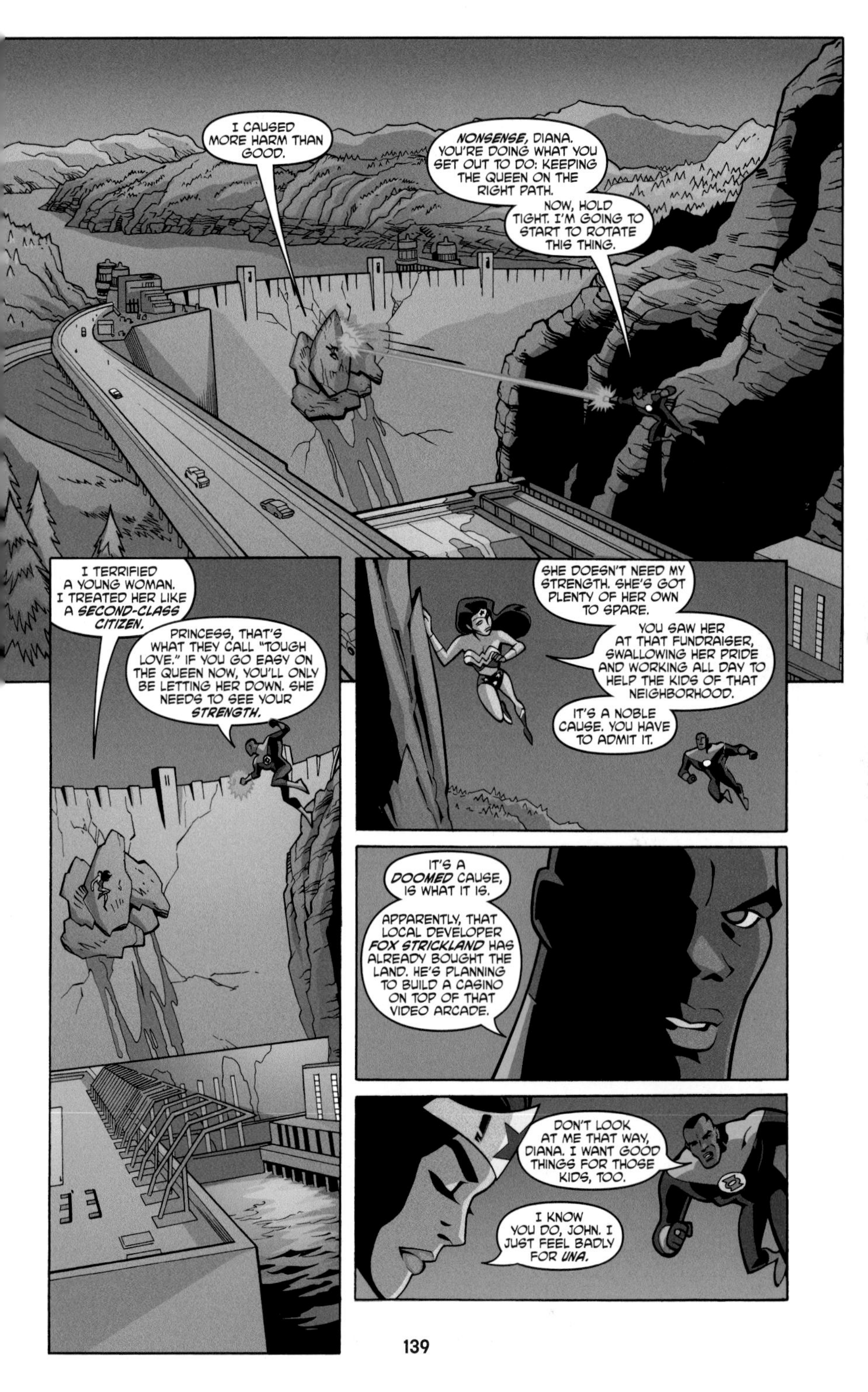
I CAUSED MORE HARM THAN GOOD.
NONSENSE, DIANA. YOU'RE DOING WHAT YOU SET OUT TO DO: KEEPING THE QUEEN ON THE RIGHT PATH.
NOW, HOLD TIGHT. I'M GOING TO START TO ROTATE THIS THING.
I TERRIFIED A YOUNG WOMAN. I TREATED HER LIKE A SECOND-CLASS CITIZEN.
PRINCESS, THAT'S WHAT THEY CALL "TOUGH LOVE." IF YOU GO EASY ON THE QUEEN NOW, YOU'LL ONLY BE LETTING HER DOWN. SHE NEEDS TO SEE YOUR STRENGTH.
SHE DOESN'T NEED MY STRENGTH. SHE'S GOT PLENTY OF HER OWN TO SPARE.
YOU SAW HER AT THAT FUNDRAISER, SWALLOWING HER PRIDE AND WORKING ALL DAY TO HELP THE KIDS OF THAT NEIGHBORHOOD.
IT'S A NOBLE CAUSE. YOU HAVE TO ADMIT IT.
IT'S A DOOMED CAUSE, IS WHAT IT IS.
APPARENTLY, THAT LOCAL DEVELOPER FOX STRICKLAND HAS ALREADY BOUGHT THE LAND. HE'S PLANNING TO BUILD A CASINO ON TOP OF THAT VIDEO ARCADE.
DON'T LOOK AT ME THAT WAY, DIANA. I WANT GOOD THINGS FOR THOSE KIDS, TOO.
I KNOW YOU DO, JOHN. I JUST FEEL BADLY FOR UNA.

RING
HELLO.
IT'S ME. TURN ON THE LOCAL NEWS.
I'M SORRY, UNA. I GUESS STRICKLAND'S MOVING AHEAD WITH HIS PLAN. AT LEAST IT'S A *CASINO*, HUH? AT LEAST HE'S NOT PUTTING IN MORE VIDEO GAMES.
FOX STRICKLAND, EMPIRE BUILDER
...KING.
YEAH?
THE JOB. DEAL ME *IN.*
THAT'S MY PAL.

THE NEXT DAY...
ALL RIGHT, GANG! WE'RE PLAYING FOR HIGH STAKES!
ARCADE
DORK TOWER
GAMES
CONNIE'S

THIS SHOULD EVEN THE SCORE A LITTLE.
WAIT A MINUTE...
YOU!
YOU!

HOW ARE WE DOING? THIS ALL GOING ACCORDING TO *PLAN?*
BUH-BUH-BUH-BUH...
BECAUSE I WOULD *HATE* FOR ANYTHING TO GO WRONG WITH SUCH A *PERFECT* SCHEME.
YOU SEE WHERE SHE--?
NO. WHAT THE HECK IS--
WARP
VEGA
SHOOOOM

ARE YOU IDIOTS GOING TO BREAK MY HEART AND SURRENDER QUIETLY?
IT'S NOT WORTH IT, KING. TELL YOUR BOYS TO--
SHE MUSTA SEEN 'EM COMING!
SET 'EM UP!
NICE.
IF WE CAN KEEP THESE BUMS LOOKING THIS WAY, QUEEN'LL GET AWAY FOR SURE!
ZONE TROOPERS

STRANGE, I NEVER CAUGHT A GLIMPSE OF THE QUEEN. MAYBE THESE FOUR WERE WORKING ALONE?

THANK THE GODS. UNA MUST HAVE GONE STRAIGHT, AFTER ALL.

EH? IS THAT WHO I THINK IT IS?
OH, NO...
WE UNDERSTAND EACH OTHER, STRICKLAND?
YOU SCRATCH MY BACK, AND I'LL SCRATCH YOUR NAME OFF THE LIST OF PEOPLE I'M GOING TO BURN TO CINDERS.

GREAT HERA! UNA...QUEEN! WHAT HAVE YOU DONE?
NOTHING. HE'S FINE. I'LL COME ALONG QUIETLY, WONDER WOMAN.
GUESS YOU WERE WRONG ABOUT ME ALL THIS TIME.

ALL'S WELL THAT ENDS WELL, I GUESS.
WHAT? THIS DIDN'T END WELL, GREEN LANTERN! THAT BUILDING WILL NEED TO BE CONDEMNED, AND A WOMAN'S *SOUL* WAS...WAS...
WHAT? *LOST?* DON'T BE SO DRAMATIC.
JOHN'S
WHAT?
SHE DIDN'T SMOKE THAT DEVELOPER GUY, DID SHE?
WAY I LOOK AT IT, THE *ROYAL FLUSH GANG* JUST DID A LITTLE *URBAN RENEWAL*, THAT'S ALL.
NOBODY EVEN GOT HURT, AND A DANGEROUS PACK OF FELONS HAVE FOLDED.
EVERYBODY *WINS.*
NOT *UNA HITCHENS*, JOHN. SHE WAS ON THE EDGE OF A REAL *REDEMPTION*. SHE WAS A FUNCTIONING MEMBER OF SOCIETY. A SUICIDE SLUM GIRL WHO WAS *BETTERING* HERSELF AND BETTERING HER *COMMUNITY*.
NOW SHE'S BACK IN *JAIL*. ALONG WITH HER TEAM OF LOWLIFE REPROBATES. ALL OF THEM SURE TO GROW BITTER AND ROT, SURROUNDED BY OTHER FELONS...OTHER LOST SOULS.
YOU KNOW WHAT YOUR PROBLEM IS, DIANA? *UNREALISTIC EXPECTATIONS.*
ME, I KNOW *SCUM* WHEN I SEE IT.
UNA HITCHENS IS A *BAD* SEED. SELFISH, DISORDERLY AND DESTRUCTIVE. JAIL CAN ONLY DO HER *GOOD.*

BACK SO SOON, QUEEN? WHAT, DID YOU MISS US SO BAD?
PROPERTY DEPOSIT
STAND BEHIND YELLOW LINE

IT'S AN UGLY OLD WORLD OUT THERE, CLANCY. I-- HEY!
COULD YOU TURN UP THAT TV?

WELL, AFTER THE... DESTRUCTION OF MY LASER ARCADE, IT'S NOW CLEAR THAT I HAVE TWO VACANT LOTS IN THE HEART OF SUICIDE SLUM. MY... UH...
...MY PLANS FOR A BIG NEW CASINO SEEM SO FOOLISH NOW. AH... I MEAN...
...WELL, LET'S JUST SAY THAT WHAT THAT NEIGHBORHOOD REALLY NEEDS IS A GIANT COMMUNITY CENTER, BUILT ON BOTH PARCELS OF LAND.
OH, AND A CHILDCARE PLACE.
AND A HEALTH CLINIC! I'M NOT FORGETTING THE HEALTH CLINIC, BELIEVE ME!
HEH.
COULDN'T CALL MY BLUFF THEN.
GOOD DEAL.
END

Whatever's on that thumb drive, you are not about to get away with it, Cheetah. You're surrounded.
Yes, release the driving thumbs!
Ha! You'll have to catch me first!

COUGH!
COUGH!
COUGH!

I've got you!
Oh? Do you?

BAM!

But how did you—? You were just—?! I had you!

I'll knock the spots right off you!

More like you'll be seeing spots. Ha ha ha! Rawwwr!

Tuo nrad tops!

POOF
Ta da!

What? Weren't expecting an encore performance?